The Secret Talker

The Secret Talker

Talker

A Novel

Geling Yan

Translated from the Chinese by Jeremy Tiang

HarperVia

An Imprint of HarperCollins*Publishers*

THE SECRET TALKER. Copyright © 2004 by San Min Book Co., Ltd. English language translation copyright © 2021 by Jeremy Tiang. All rights reserved. Printed in the United States of America. No part of this book may be used or reproduced in any manner whatsoever without written permission except in the case of brief quotations embodied in critical articles and reviews. For information, address HarperCollins Publishers, 195 Broadway, New York, NY 10007.

HarperCollins books may be purchased for educational, business, or sales promotional use. For information, please email the Special Markets Department at SPsales@harpercollins.com.

FIRST EDITION

Designed by SBI Book Arts, LLC

Library of Congress Cataloging-in-Publication Data has been applied for.

ISBN 978-0-06-300403-0

21 22 23 24 25 LSC 10 9 8 7 6 5 4 3 2 1

The Secret
Talker

1

This stranger on the internet was asking Qiao Hongmei if she remembered him. He said he had watched her walk into the restaurant with a tall American man. She'd stood there with her arms loosely folded, weight on one leg, the picture of indifference. She'd been face-to-face with him for half a minute, waiting for the hostess. In those thirty seconds, he'd smirked at her. His seat had faced the door, and he'd reckoned she shouldn't be deprived of his smile. He'd been holding an open menu, ready to order, when he heard her say in her foreign accent, "Thank God it's not too crowded."

He'd looked up, and there she was, Qiao Hongmei. And so he'd shot her an admiring grin. Very few people could resist his smile. Men or women, friends or strangers, all fell prey to his high-wattage, unerring smile. Well, that's what he told her.

Hongmei had to stop reading for a moment. This stranger evidently had taken note of her every move and gesture the night before. His tone was a little presumptuous, but she liked his writing style, almost like a blend of Neil Gaiman and Emily Brontë.

He said that as Hongmei had followed her husband to a table by the windows, he had smelled the floral aroma wafting off her long hair. Her eyes had dropped demurely as she passed each table, perhaps checking out the food, perhaps the diners' faces, before she'd turned around and looked straight at him. He reckoned staring too hard at someone made them sense danger, particularly a perceptive woman like her. He said she looked twenty-eight, thirty at most, though he knew she was older. Hongmei had glanced around, her eyes alighting momentarily on his face. At least he thought they had, this internet Romeo.

He'd watched as her husband had helped her take off her coat, stroking her cheek as he did so. She'd flinched a little, and he'd noticed that too. That was great, he said. It showed her skin wasn't numb yet; she was still capable of rejecting a meaningless caress. He asked if she had designed her own outfit—long trousers in a soft, wrinkled hemp fabric and alarmingly sexy beaded sandals that left her feet almost naked, light dancing through the nearly colorless crystals.

She shuddered, goose bumps rising. She looked around her study, then down at her feet beneath the desk. Were they that revealing? Could feet be seductive too? It seemed so. The crystals on the thin straps of her sandals glistened like dew, like sweat. Her husband had never asked how those beads had gone from the bedroom curtains to her feet, where their hints of sensuality were now there for anyone who could detect them. She pretended not to have any views on this, but he'd seen right through her.

Then there was her blouse. He thought that had been excellent too, its threads changing color with the light. Your handiwork? he asked, so rude, so imaginative.

Next he wanted to discuss her husband. A clever-looking man, he said, and full of energy. A little old, certainly, but not bad on the whole, very suited to her. On the whole, in everyone's eyes. Apart from him—he could see past the whole.

Here we go, she thought. *Sowing dissent.*

But none of that mattered, right? he went on. His tone was a little dictatorial but also a little poetic, even affectionate. What woman would put up with this, sentiment hidden beneath a layer of meanness?

The important thing, he said, was that Hongmei was completely closed off from her husband—sorry, this was where he had to talk about her "soul." He wanted her forgiveness for using such a corny term, and he assured her he wasn't the sort of guy who tossed around words like that. It wasn't just her husband she was closed off from; her soul was also shut off from its surroundings.

I'm not trying to make trouble between you, he added, definitely not.

That's exactly what you're doing, she thought.

Her husband was a man who liked to joke—you could tell that at a glance—but he wrongly believed that as long as he could make his wife laugh, everything was all right. When her husband had delivered a punch line, this man had watched as Hongmei threw back her head and guffawed, but he could tell she had been distracted. The husband had chortled so hard his face had turned bright red, but as for her, she had shot an accusatory sideways look at him, to show she'd been mildly offended by his harmless dirty joke, just like every middle-class wife of the intelligentsia, just like every helpless woman from a good American family, deriving a flash of pleasure from the heavy-handed, inescapable smuttiness of men while pretending to admonish them.

He knew she had been faking. He said he'd never met a woman so good at pretending as Hongmei. As far as her husband was concerned, she was a secret talker, every breath, bite, and laugh part of the enigma. That's why this man was so fascinated by her. Then he abruptly changed the subject, as though he was suddenly aware of how strange, how creepy Hongmei might find him, assuring her that it was both coincidence and inevitability that had led him to her email address, and she shouldn't be alarmed.

Hongmei started clacking away at the keyboard, to say she wasn't alarmed, though she felt there were too many people playing this game, and she wasn't interested. It wasn't hard to guess how he'd gotten her email address. Between her school and the library, her many friends and acquaintances, he could have found it without too much trouble. She got spam trying to sell her plane tickets, phone cards, CDs, books, secondhand stuff—and she'd never asked how they got her email, whether by fair means or foul. She told him that when she opened her inbox each day, nine out of ten messages were from glib strangers like him, hawking high-interest loans or tax loopholes, offering debt evasion or cut-price jewelry, skin creams, X-rated entertainment, male escorts, or hookers. Why should she be alarmed?

She hid her slight attraction to this mysterious man beneath a layer of banter. Then she thanked him for his flattery.

He replied right away, saying it was strange she'd taken his words for flattery. He hadn't praised her beauty, and actually didn't even think she was pretty. In English, "fascinated" just meant a single-minded curiosity—that was all. He felt the same thing for death-row convicts and clownish politicians.

Hongmei was surprised. Many people said she was pretty. How dare this person insult her! Her eyes sought out the words "alarmingly sexy," which had made her heartbeat quicken, but now his tone seemed indifferent, objective, even dismissive. She thought about how his casual humiliation of her abruptly shortened the distance between them. All of a sudden he was believable, solidly present. How cheap she was, wanting to talk to him just because he'd pricked her vanity.

Her fingers started drumming again. Thank you for your frankness, she wrote. Unfortunately, I'm not in the habit of discussing myself with a stranger. She read it over and deleted the second sentence. Better. Cool and composed. He'd read these words and see how she'd turned the tables on him, with the understatement of an old hand. The message was clear: *Come on, then. Let's see who gets under whose skin first.*

The stranger's response was swift, claiming he didn't regard frankness as a virtue.

You're not frank at all, you riddle of a woman.

A challenge. She stood up, trying to suppress the excitement she felt in that moment. So she had a combative streak in her. By calling her a riddle, he became one himself. As far as Hongmei was concerned, he was the true secret talker, messaging her from the shadows and keeping his identity hidden while he judged her, exposed her.

She picked up her mug, only to find herself gulping air. It was empty. She had to calm down. This man who knew nothing about her had managed to reach her, climbing along the vine of the internet cable. He'd bypassed her husband, Glen, and barged straight into the 150 square feet of her study.

Qiao Hongmei stood before the mirror, posing the way he'd described her, with her weight on one leg. She tried desperately to remember who'd been in the restaurant the night before, but not a single face remained in her mind. Yet he existed. A stranger's existence, gradually taking on form and substance, a hint of bodily warmth, in their sixteenth-floor apartment with her unwitting husband in the next room.

Hongmei walked out of her study and into the kitchen, clutching her empty mug. She looked up suddenly to see Glen in a tracksuit. He was going for a jog, he said, and they could have breakfast together when he got back.

"All right," she said. "Enjoy your run."

His dark brown eyes lingered on her face.

"What is it?" she asked.

He said, "It's good. You look very well."

"You too," she said.

Just as she was about to go back into her study, the door opened again and Glen thrust a FedEx package through the crack. She took the parcel, which felt like a couple of books. The best thing about Glen being a professor was his book purchases were tax-deductible; he got an order every couple of days. She tossed the package across the coffee table onto the couch, but it landed on the floor. Ignoring it, she went back into her study, then felt that wasn't very nice of her, returned, and picked up the package. Her water sloshed onto Glen's beloved Native American rug, its red dye apparently made from crushed bugs.

— — —

Back at her computer, she sipped her ice water. Twenty minutes later, his reply arrived. He said Hongmei probably wanted to know what he was like. He was five foot nine (not particularly tall), 185 pounds (just the way she liked it), with black hair and eyes. About himself: majored in English at Yale, got his master's at Harvard, then dropped out after one year of working toward a PhD. The money his father left him was doing well in the hands of an investment broker. He and Hongmei were the same; they both found it hard to be faithful to a single person or profession. The instant he had set eyes on her, he had sighed that fidelity of the flesh was the easiest kind, and therefore the least important.

Qiao Hongmei read line after line of this revealing introduction and felt like this man was filming himself in close-up. Not his face, but his breath. She grew more captivated, even as she remained eighty percent skeptical about the existence of the wealthy father and impressive academic record. Are you suggesting that I'm unfaithful? she said.

He replied: I'm not suggesting anything; I'm pointing out your infidelity. I think you're an intelligent woman who understands that we don't need to worry about the word "faithful." Your soul has never been faithful, not for a single minute. Then he apologized again, for using a specious word like "soul."

She said: Fine, anything you say; I can be unfaithful. She leaned back in her chair, unwilling to explain further.

The man changed the subject, saying, Don't be like that. That's how you are with everyone else; don't be like that with me. We need to have a good beginning.

He'd gone too far now. Hongmei was turned off by this sudden intimacy. He sensed this right away, writing: Don't misunderstand; I'll give you plenty of time to get used to me, before we have any sort of beginning. A few minutes passed. Without being aware of it, she'd started gnawing at her nails. He sent another couple of lines, asking her to relax, not to be so scared, or he'd abandon this date right away. He actually used the word "date." Hongmei contemplated it. He said he just wanted to understand her. Since she wouldn't have chewed her nails into such an awful state unless there was a reason.

Hongmei reflexively clenched her hands into fists. He had even noticed her bitten nails! Or had she been chewing

them in the restaurant? No, she generally didn't in public places. Besides, before leaving the house with Glen, she'd stuck on some rather convincing fake nails. That's what she usually did when going to a swanky place. The fakes weren't too long, looked healthy and clean, not the gaudy ones sported by receptionists or the Taylor Street hookers. Yet he had said she must've had a reason to chew her nails like that.

She tapped away with one hand, deleting and rewriting, asking how long he'd been following her—she didn't believe last night was the first time he'd seen her. He declined to answer.

Even though she was excited, Hongmei felt her hair stand on end. She said biting her nails was a bad habit left over from childhood.

He said he'd soon find out the real cause.

Don't you try that—one glance at me and you think you can magically see into me, she thought. On the computer, she asked him how many women he was sending these messages to. He didn't deny it, didn't claim he spoke to only her in this way. He said at the moment there were no other suitable candidates for him to chat with. She asked what he meant by "suitable candidates." He said a woman like her, extremely reserved and extremely discontented.

Hongmei thought "discontented" was about right.

He said yesterday, at the restaurant, he'd been studying

her all along. To her right had been a stainless-steel radiator that had reflected her profile. He had been able to see what her hand was doing on that side, pushing the hair back from her face, gently rubbing her temples, fiddling with her clear crystal earring, stirring her drink with her straw. She had looked impatient, bored, but other people would have read this as elegance and refinement. He even described her expression, calling her eyes inviting.

Inviting people's attention?

Not just that. He said her eyes had been asking to be caressed, truly caressed. They wanted others to look back at them, to feel. Maybe they even wanted to be invaded, to be conquered and possessed. He'd never encountered such an ambivalent woman. He believed it was in this moment that she'd captured him.

A knock at the door. Before she could react, Glen thrust his face in, flushed and sweaty. She asked if he'd had a good run.

"Unbelievably good," he said. "Now let's have breakfast."

She said, "I'll be there in a minute."

Glen said, "Wow. You look stunning this morning. Your eyes are ablaze." With that, his lanky body leaned over the desk, his lips pursed. This was the obligatory morning kiss, and God help her if she tried to get out of it.

Hongmei pressed her lips to his right away and stood up. The only way to get him out of here at once was to go have breakfast. Her diversionary tactic worked, and Glen didn't so much as glance at the words on the screen. With his arm around her waist, they headed for the kitchen. Beneath his palm, his errant Asian wife, she imagined, felt young and demure, absolutely perfect.

And behind them was the evidence of her flirtation with a strange man.

— — —

The man showed up in her inbox again three days later. Giving her enough time to miss him. He said sorry for not being around; his only daughter had come for a surprise visit, and those three days had been all hers. He hadn't seen her in twelve years, and every one of the birthday cards he'd mailed her had been returned.

Hongmei deduced that this meant he was at least forty-five. Men these days became fathers around the age of thirty. She asked why his daughter had returned his birthday presents, and he said, She kept the gifts; it was just the cards she sent back. The presents were repackaged and passed off as being from someone else. A gift is still a gift. His tone was dispassionate, not overblown, but she could sense how hurt he was. For a moment, he lost a great deal of his anonymity. There was nothing vague about being hurt—these wounds could cause two people to identify with each other, no matter how different they were. Being in contact with this thoroughly unreliable man, his injury suddenly made him seem dependable.

She asked if his daughter looked like him. He said her hair was like her mother's, but otherwise she was exactly like him. She said she must be little and delicate, perhaps she was mixed-race.

He saw the trap and said he hated mixed-race girls.

Hongmei felt surprised by the vehemence in his words, at odds with his all-knowing aloofness. She had finally struck a chord.

No point trying to guess my ethnicity or learn anything about me, he said. We're fated never to meet.

Fated?

Fated.

2

It was late at night. She could hear music playing in Glen's room. He needed accompaniment when reading or writing. At this moment it was Charlotte Church singing. A voice like peppermint. In this explosive world, thank God for being able to dip into the peppermint of Charlotte Church's voice.

She and the man studied each other silently, one in this patch of night, one somewhere else.

He said he'd sent his daughter off on an airplane that afternoon and missed her right away. He didn't know why this would be. Maybe his daughter's inapproachability was also only on the surface, and her heart was docile beneath the surface.

She asked him, Do you think I'm one way on the surface and another way inside?

He said anyone with her demure exterior, her quiet smile, would be the same. In the restaurant, he'd seen her accept a menu, then order without glancing at it. He'd watched as her husband ordered her both white and red wine, and she'd nodded and smiled, placidly accepting. And her feet? Those nearly bare feet had been tapping out a beat, to a secret melody. She had been secretly amusing herself.

She asked if he was an expert in psychology or perhaps behavioral studies.

He said, You don't need to worry about me being idle, and don't waste your time trying to guess whether I have a proper profession. I don't do anything, yet I do everything. You'll find out about it. We're meeting soon, aren't we?

Hongmei had no idea. Hadn't he recently said they were fated never to meet? Did she want to meet him? What would that mean? She could still hear, through the wall, Charlotte Church's pure voice. Glen was working late. Probably waiting up for his hardworking wife, hoping she'd want to make love later.

She wrote, That's enough for tonight. My husband's waiting. I have to go to bed.

He said, All right. So you're generous with your body— very pure of you. I wish you pleasure.

What right does he have to be jealous? Hongmei laughed to herself.

He asked when their next date could be.

She said there wouldn't be a next date, online or otherwise. That was a snap decision. Not giving him a chance to respond, she typed quickly, saying her husband loved her very much, and they'd destroyed their reputations to be together. This was what the Chinese called nine deaths, one life—a narrow escape. She couldn't have this sort of liaison behind his back.

She said, Thank you for your concern, and thank you for making the effort to understand me.

Then she swiftly logged off and shut down the computer. For a while, she couldn't muster the energy to stand up, and even raising her hand to the light switch was difficult. In the instant between light and dark, she glimpsed a woman's silhouette and almost let out a scream of terror. Turning the lamp on again, she realized it was her own reflection in the mirror. It was her own fault for having a mirror in the study. She'd never been so unfamiliar to herself—face red and greasy, eyes moist, looking dazed. And her lips, and her breasts—this was probably how women always looked when their flesh was transgressing. It was preemptively showing on her face and body. Her body had moved ahead of her—how unthinkable. She had to uproot whatever stray tendril had allowed this secret talker to creep his way in.

She sat heavily back in the swivel chair, planting her feet on the floor and pulling herself back to the desk to turn on her computer again. When she opened her inbox, his reply was waiting. What kind of response would this be? She decided not to read it. Surely it would just be even more persuasive language to demonstrate how much he understood her. Or else he'd try to nag her (saying she wasn't pretty or something like that, to make her want him), and then say, Hey, what are you thinking? I don't want to be your lover; I didn't ask you to betray your husband. I don't even like mixed-race girls, let alone a fully Asian woman like you.

Whatever he said, she wasn't going to fall into his trap.

One second later, she was staring at his reply. It contained only one word, in English: Fine.

So that was that. A crisp, clear response: Fine. And with that, he would stop pestering her. She glared at the word. Had he really given up? He hadn't lost any dignity, probably even delivered this with a cold, proud smile: Fine. Maybe sorrow in his eyes. Or maybe not; maybe he thought this was funny—amused by women who make a big deal out of nothing. Just a shrug, Fine, and he walked away, perhaps with some regret, but his self-control was absolute, not to mention his manners. Hands stuck in his pockets, the wind ruffling his full head of dark hair, walking away with forceful, measured steps. A slowly receding silhouette.

Hongmei hadn't expected such a quick retreat. She was being a killjoy. She didn't know what she was afraid of. A playboy had walked away and would surely be moving right on to his next conquest, leaving her in peace and quiet.

— — —

After three days of quiet, his messages started coming again. She read them, line by line. He mainly wrote about his daughter and their three days together. There was true fatherliness in those simple words. For three days he'd studied his quiet daughter with unbelieving eyes, saying he felt sorry for her, then suddenly realizing from her silent smile that he'd already said this to her, perhaps more than once. When she was just an infant, he used to hold her in the night and carry her up and down, from the first floor up to the fourth, so as not to wake her mother and the neighbors. He had known her so well back then, when she needed food, a hug, or her diaper changed. Now the girl looked at him with a mysterious expression, hiding her true feelings. She was unreadable, suddenly bursting into giggles. Laughing at how pathetic he was—every father has such riveting memories. Or perhaps she was remembering her mother's words, that her father's only investment in her was a single sperm. He took his daughter to see some famous landmarks, taking endless photos, buying her jewelry and handicrafts from Fisherman's Wharf, bringing her to a Napa spa for a massage, getting her an expensive outfit that her gaze had lingered over merely a moment. And still he could see in his daughter's smile that he was thoroughly pitiful, no more than a single sperm, a groveling, free-spending giant sperm.

Hongmei imagined his daughter as a child of fourteen. She saw this long-limbed girl vanishing into the dimness of the boarding gate, and the man abruptly realizing what sort of creature he was, someone who hassled strange women over email, someone who sat alone in restaurants or coffee shops, quietly waiting for prey like Hongmei. Perhaps as he'd driven home from the airport, he'd had a change of heart, all because of his daughter.

— — —

Late that night, she and Glen made love. It was better than it had been in a long time. As if she was using Glen to express her passion for someone else, or perhaps Glen had somehow become unfamiliar, a stranger. Then she rolled over and went to sleep, though of course she was only pretending. She was afraid Glen would speak, breaking the spell.

For the next week, Hongmei didn't check her email. The man had vanished just like that. Her bad habit of biting her nails came back. She discovered that she wasn't doing this out of anxiety but the opposite: the calm of having nothing to hope for.

On the eighth day, she sent him a message asking him to suggest a few recent books on psychology. She avoided mentioning the unfortunate ending of their last conversation and the yearning she'd felt these last few days.

No reply.

Three days later, she sent the same message again, adding a line to explain that she was afraid the last email had gone astray and never reached him.

Still no reply. She abandoned her pride and bombarded him with messages.

Chewing her nails, Hongmei thought he must be a gentleman after all, to keep his word like this. Perhaps the soul he was so against mentioning was no longer empty, now that his long-lost daughter had resurfaced to fill it. For whatever reason, he was determined to ignore her, which left Hongmei at a loss. What was he doing now? Sitting at his computer, mockingly watching her sink into despair and disappointment. Her hair a mess and her nails ruined as she took up the banner of studying again in a bid to wrest back his attention and cling on to it. Her fake respectability and reluctance to be alone must've been hugely amusing to him. That's how he wanted to write her—an easily seduced woman had to be considered on such harsh terms.

After another two days of waiting, Hongmei calmed down and felt a little ashamed of herself. She started catching up on the schoolwork she'd missed and paid close attention when Glen was talking.

Listening carefully to Glen paid dividends. He mentioned

that in class he was always asking his students to pay attention to Kafka's use of the first person. "*The Metamorphosis* appears to be written in the third person, but actually it's the first, apart from the final section, after Gregor-the-insect has died." He said choosing the right perspective was the biggest factor in a novel's success. "If *The Catcher in the Rye* hadn't been in the first person, it would have failed utterly. If Michel Butor hadn't written in the second person, his would have been an entirely third-rate work."

Hongmei noticed a crumb of bread in the corner of his mouth. The first sign of aging was how it took such a long time to eat anything. She responded, "Emails are always in the second person."

Glen said, "We generally use the third person when we're talking to ourselves, discussing something. So if someone's having a long conversation with you online, that's the same as you speaking to yourself."

Hongmei thought, *Glen's clever after all*, as if she'd just noticed.

After the emails had stopped, the image of the secret talker had grown clearer. Black hair, black eyes, the sort of smile that was always mocking his own romantic tendencies. She would forget him. How many encounters of this sort does a woman have in her life? Everyone's been through these short-lived infatuations.

3

On the twenty-fifth day after he'd said fine, Hongmei got another email. He said she'd walked into the library looking like a lost child. His guess was that her eyes had been adjusting to the indoor gloom, or else she had been searching for a better place to sit and read. He said she'd stood there, lost, for quite a while. There was an instant when he'd almost surrendered, certain that she'd recognized him, her vague impression from the restaurant suddenly clicking with a face in the library. He'd been about to stand up from his carrel, but she was already moving toward the desks, the tassels on her homemade cloth bag swaying vivaciously. He said that of the five bags he'd seen her carry this was the prettiest.

She was startled. So this man had never left her, not for a single day. He wasn't as tragic as he'd presented himself, riding off alone like a classical knight. Rather, he was like a ghost, secretly taking part in her life, undetected.

He'd seen her walk along a row of desks, and as she'd squeezed into the innermost seat, her right knee had bumped against the table. He'd heard the thud. A bruise larger than the palm of a year-old child, he guessed. At these words, Hongmei stood and shut the study door, then raised her nightgown inch by inch. Sure enough, there was a dark purple patch above her right knee. She stared at it, thinking back to that afternoon in the library. She'd arrived at a downtime, when most of the students were yawning away, the older ones not even lifting their heads from the desks.

How had this person inserted himself among them?

He said he'd spent much of his childhood, adolescence, and adulthood in libraries, like Borges, except he didn't write stories. He said he'd thought he was strong enough to break it off. He didn't want to disturb Hongmei or himself. It was unfortunate that people had desires—he hoped Hongmei agreed with this point. She could prevent him from writing, but she couldn't stop his obsession.

Waves of hot and cold spread over Hongmei's body. Twenty-odd days of silence made him seem haggard when he reappeared, eyes dark with passion, but still as collected as ever, she dumbly imagined. She took her image of the ideal man and laid it on top of him.

He said, Please don't reply—anything you say would only hurt me.

She wrote back right away, saying she was very happy to be talking with him again. Before she could press SEND, she felt uneasy and changed it to: Very glad to hear all's well with you.

Five minutes later, he responded to say Hongmei was exactly the same as his daughter, always so careful not to reveal her true feelings, forcing him to sift through the haystack of her emotions. His daughter had departed so many days ago, and the only thing she'd written him since then was: Very glad to hear all's well with you. He said, The pair of you seem to know better how well I am than I do myself.

Hongmei said, You seem disappointed.

The man said, Disppointment is my usual state.

She abruptly noticed that he'd spelled "disappoint-ment" incorrectly—missing an *a*. Could it be that he was a foreigner? Say, Italian, Greek, or even Russian?

He asked where she'd bought that long blue dress with the white pattern; it looked utterly foreign.

She told him this was called pattern-print cloth, a hand-icraft from the village she'd grown up in. Every woman in this place used to know how to weave this fabric, and on rainy days if you walked down the paved road between the rural dwellings, you'd hear shuttles clacking as the looms worked away. She didn't realize she was already starting to disclose her origins, her history, to this man. In the picture she presented him, the Jiangnan village she'd once despised became beautiful. She showed it to him in its entirety, the black tiles and whitewashed walls, the covered boats, the endless yellow fields of rapeseed blossom. Then zooming in to a medium shot: a stone bridge with children walking across it, young cowherds on their way to work. Among them was a girl of six or seven—that was her. She'd been born in the year of the Cultural Revolution, and her illiterate parents had given her a name that was trendy at the time: 红梅, Hongmei, red plum blossom. She'd wanted to change this country-bumpkin-sounding name on a few occasions but couldn't bring herself to do it. After all, her parents had raised her only once, named her only once.

He replied that he could see this remote riverside village. It sounds like you love it a lot, don't you? That's the only way you would describe it in those terms.

She was startled. She'd never thought she loved it; in fact she'd wanted above all to get away from it. When meeting new people, she lied about it, trying to keep it hidden. She'd once thought anywhere was better than her village, that back-of-beyond place, as out of touch as a frog at the bottom of a well. As a young child, she'd encountered a group of people known as "educated youths," city kids sent to the countryside under the Red Guards' watchful eyes, who had confirmed her instincts—they had done nothing but criticize the place. Just like her, they had thought nowhere on this Earth could be so hideous. How could she love it?

Hongmei said, You're probably going to be disappointed again—I've worked hard all my life to get as far from that village as possible. I left that place for the last time nine years ago and made up my mind never to go back. The day I left, when I walked past the commemorative plaque by the entrance, for some reason I stopped and read it. Two hundred thirteen girls died in a single night. I'd never looked at their names properly. The year after they passed away, my mother came into this world. That winter only female babies were born, as if to make up for the dead ones. I said those names out loud, each as unsophisticated as my own. My aunt was the sixth one, and my great-aunts were numbers eighty and eighty-one. All the girls, with only three surnames between them, aged between six and eighteen, had died on one night.

Those young women, who were called "dead losses" while they were alive, were all murdered on a rainy night in November 1937. Even the Japanese troops were stunned into silence. They entered the village that evening, searching every home for Chinese soldiers, food, and young women. Only old people and young boys were left. One of the men lost his temper and stabbed his bayonet into a haystack—

Hang on, have I told you about our village haystacks? Many good things, bad things, terrifying things took place beneath those haystacks. They stood there all year round and knew many secrets: shameful relationships, family rivalries, unavoidable abortions. The blade came out, and everything changed. There was fresh blood on it, faintly emitting steam in the early winter night. He stabbed again, and this time the blood dripped off the silver blade. Yet the haystack didn't so much as quiver, didn't let out a single sound.

Ten minutes later, the Japanese soldiers had surrounded all twenty-odd haystacks and were plunging their bayonets in on all sides. All came out bloodied, yet the piles of hay remained quiet, without even a single straw shaking. The interpreter started yelling, saying, "Come out quick if you want to live; we're setting these on fire." No movement, no words. The haystacks could swallow any number of secrets and wouldn't let anything back out. Gasoline was splashed onto them, and the flames roared like lions and tigers. The Japanese troops leaned on their rifles, watching as the hay turned gold, then red, and finally black, wisps of gray ash quivering in the remains, dancing in an icy gale. The air smelled of burned flesh. The soldiers, starved for many days, bent over and threw up bile. They didn't have to look any closer to understand the results of this massacre. They weren't pleased with themselves at all but for some reason felt angry, distressed, frightened. In the end, they weren't even brave enough to tear open the smoking mounds but quietly wiped the still-wet blood off their bayonets. All the girls in the village had been exterminated. They had been prepared for that, but the resignation and silence with which these girls had accepted death stunned the Japanese out of their wits. They gave up their plans to pillage and torture the rest of the villagers, and simply departed. This was the most bizarre act of resistance they encountered during the entire invasion.

At this point, Hongmei found her eyes too swollen with tears to see the words clearly. She'd never imagined she could be so proud of her village. These more than two hundred young women who'd given up their lives had not affected her so much till this moment, nor had she found their sacrifice this meaningful. Was she endowing them with significance? Or had this already been present but she'd only just discovered it?

The man's only response was: I have no words in the face of such a story.

She wanted to tell him that she'd never shared this history with anyone, not even her husband. No idea why. Perhaps until she'd understood its meaning, it had been only one of many stories about the Chinese resistance. She'd never told

Glen because she'd lied to him, as she had to so many others. She always invented a birthplace—Inner Mongolia or Tibet, far better than this ignorant, closed-off village. She'd told Glen she was from the Yellow Mountains, hoping that imposing landscape would erase the pettiness of her little village.

Yet now she had stopped lying and told this man everything about her village. After all the girls had been killed, the attitude toward female children changed completely, and they were no longer known as "dead losses." The two hundred thirteen sacrificial victims became the villagers' spirit guardians. Women were then revered over men, so girls were sent away to the city for school, while boys were exploited for their physical strength—once again demonstrating the narrow-minded foolishness of these people. Gradually, the women drifted away, moving on to bigger and better things. Girls who studied in the city rarely came back to marry village boys. Hongmei had been one of those girls. Her mother's family had been too poor to send her away, and so her mother's one wish had been to give her daughter the education she'd missed out on.

The man said, I wish I could see you now, your eyes full of homesickness, a pang of guilt in your heart. You find it strange to be so moved. You're embarrassed; you've turned your face aside.

Hongmei wrote, Thank you for your patience, listening

to me tell a story millions of miles removed from you. I know Americans don't like tragedies. My husband doesn't.

Then she thought, *No, that's not right.* What was this? Criticizing Glen in front of this man?

So she deleted that last sentence.

4

It was four in the afternoon when Hongmei entered the library. First she went in the direction of the restrooms. Two drinking fountains, one tall and one short. She chose the shorter one. The water formed a perfect arc, which her lips disrupted. Her eyes swung around—no one was following her. She turned to the left, dabbing at the water droplets on her mouth and cheeks with a Kleenex. Six people in sight, but none of them could be him—too young. She'd already covered one-fifth of the library's area. There were fewer than a hundred thousand people on campus, and she was always running into familiar faces in the library. She kept walking, as if searching for someone, though she could equally have been looking for a seat. Another fifth. Including her walk from the entrance to the drinking fountain, she'd covered more than half the room. She stopped and quickly checked if she could feel someone's attention burning into her. She thought she could.

Finding a free computer, she sat down and logged into her email.

The man said he'd seen her strolling by and tried to connect her with the story she'd told him the night before. He was starting to understand what was up with her. He said he'd never seen anyone with such a weighty, twisted love for their hometown.

Hongmei thought, *He wants to call it love—all right, then.*

He said the weightiness and twistiness gave her a distinctive bearing. Perhaps that's why he couldn't give her up. He had watched her walk across the lawn, not because he wanted to lie in wait for her but because desire had left him helpless. He had watched her leave through the glass doors of her condo, stopping for a chat on the lawn with an acquaintance walking his dog, saying the weather's so nice, hope it stays this way. Then Hongmei had patted the dog tenderly, so he could tell she got on well with animals and was comfortable around them. As she had bent to stroke the dog, her shawl had fallen on the ground. He said that shawl had made her thoughtlessly put-together outfit come together in a powerful statement. The near-extinct pattern and color had made the vast grass plain pale in comparison. The red had put him in mind of Native American rugs, made by crushing a species of bugs into fragments. Saturated, animalistic, different from any other shade of red, antiquity itself. And then Hongmei had walked on, her posture as modest and evasive as always, the stark white bourgeois condo building behind her, its sixteen stories housing more than ten of this college's professors, living their stark white lives.

So he even knew how many professors lived in her building? Hongmei looked around. A young guy nearby was laughing loudly, chatting animatedly with some unseen person. She'd heard they could have parties online, ten or more of them gabbing away, thousands of miles apart.

The man said he was surprised at himself, ruthlessly abandoning his usual ethical standards and giving in to desire, behaving in such an underhanded manner. There were several long benches around the lawn. He'd sat on one of them, and when she had been within twenty yards of him, he'd said to himself, *All right, time to make my entrance.* He only had to stand and reach out a hand. But when she was just five paces away, she suddenly had turned back to the condo and waved at a sixteenth-floor balcony. Her gesture had been mundane, just like her smile, full of the security and numbness of her present life. From his angle, he had been able to see a furled, pale blue picnic umbrella, white plastic chairs around a table, and a steaming mug. Perhaps her husband had been having his last cup of coffee for the morning. And so the man hadn't stood and started things off with her. Perhaps he wanted to wait a little longer, so the feeling of uselessness caused by desire would have a chance to dissipate. Not just desire, also vague, shameful schemes, he frankly told her.

He was afraid that if he walked out from behind the shelter of words, he wouldn't be able to control himself. Your body grants tacit consent to men, he wrote, but luckily only a very few of us are able to see this.

His language was turning creepy and Nietzschean again, she thought.

As she had passed his bench, she finished the apple she had brought and tossed the core into a trash can, pulled a Kleenex from her purse to wipe her mouth and hands. The dog walker came back, and she turned around to avoid a second bout of small talk, but her plan was foiled by the dog, which jumped up and rested its front paws on her thigh. Beneath this show of eagerness, it humped her leg. Neither she nor the owner had acknowledged this fact. Instead, they had chatted about how great the morning was!

The man was certain Hongmei had known the dog owner for many years, and the two of them were keeping a tight lid on their relationship. He said the instant Hongmei had turned from the trash can, she was a different person: conventional, reasonable, and respectful of pallid petit bourgeois friendships. Who could have imagined a woman like her coming from such a small village, one that had sacrificed two hundred thirteen girls and now sent its female inhabitants far and wide?

She told the man she was glad he'd given her the opportunity to get to know herself. The clarity of his vision, that almost supernatural intuition, made her wish for the first time to open herself up. Her secrets weren't kept just from other people but also from herself.

These secrets were tightly sealed away. The first time she had known they existed was in 1977, when she was eleven. More winter, more haystacks. Eight teenaged students from the cities, sent down to be reeducated by peasants, had departed, leaving only one, a boy of nineteen. He often would lounge atop a haystack, playing his harmonica, and when he tired of that, he would regale the village children with stories of Nanjing, Shanghai, America. He'd be talking away, then suddenly stop, sometimes halfway through a sentence. He looked bizarre at these moments, staring at them through dirty glasses out of first one eye and then the other, as if he'd just landed among them a minute ago. Then, in a completely different tone, he'd say, "You're all so lucky—if you grow up in ignorance, then you can't even tell how ignorant you are." He said that if only there could be a fire to burn up all the haystacks, then this little village that had trapped him wouldn't exist anymore. He stayed a full year after all his comrades had left, cursing and raving, his beard scraggly, lying in bed half the time, claiming to be ill. That year Hongmei the little girl heard many stories escape from his lips: Lincoln of

America, Bacon of England, Byron and Shelley. No matter what he told the kids, there was always that moment when he suddenly switched, using the topic to show how insignificant, pathetic, and uninformed this village was. Just as he was starting to resign himself to his fate, something awful happened: he was burned to death in a haystack. Several of the mounds on the threshing grounds went up in flames that night. Perhaps the fire wasn't an accident. People had seen him grabbing a village girl, more than once, and disappearing with her into the soft embrace of a haystack.

5

The village children were sad for a long time about the boy's permanent disappearance, though on the surface they appeared to hate him. Girls would hum the tunes he'd played on his harmonica, not knowing those were all Russian folk songs.

Hongmei typed, The strange thing is, you see, when I first saw Glen, I suddenly thought of this educated youth.

Now she wanted this person to see Glen as he'd first appeared to her, aged forty-nine, his sideburns stippled with white, but with the build of a young guy. At that time, everything in Hongmei's life was going well; she and her husband had finally managed to get transferred from the south to Beijing and had just been allocated living quarters. She had a stable job as a military interpreter and was taking English classes on side—that was where Glen came into the picture. Unlike the other foreign professors at her school, he had self-confidence and maturity. Glen strode into the classroom, his back ramrod straight, apparently unworried about attracting trouble with how different he was, how confident he could be. He said in Mandarin, "Good morning," then told the class the second and third phrases he'd learned in their language were "hot water" and "meat bun." He stopped there, as if waiting for something, and resumed a moment later. "Why didn't you laugh? That pause was so you could laugh." He told the students that one of his colleagues had taught in China, and when he got back to the States, he warned Glen that the most important words he'd learn were "hot water"; otherwise he'd miss the attendant coming down the corridor dispensing it each morning, and then he couldn't even have a cup of coffee. "Meat bun" was important too; otherwise the canteen staff might give him a solid steamed bun without any meat filling. He also knew one other Chinese phrase, "I love you." As the students gaped at him, he told them he'd memorized this but would certainly never say it out loud to a woman. The same colleague had warned him that if he said it to a woman, the rest of his time in China would be bloody troublesome. He actually used the British swear word "bloody," which stripped away his scholarly image right away. He told the students, particularly the cute female ones, to be sure to remind Professor Glen never to say "I love you" out loud. He was an old hand at love songs.

As she wrote these words, Hongmei realized she was

smiling at the Glen she was conjuring up. She knew how attractive he was. She told the guy, You have no idea how I felt when Glen said those three Chinese words, "I," "love," "you." They were beyond the capabilities of his mouth, and he looked like a child trying to spit them out.

Glen had licked his lips as a bold female student corrected his pronunciation. He had tried again. Hongmei had barely been able to listen. The words had been raw, tender in his mouth, precisely because she couldn't bear to hear them. So many years later, she still couldn't explain how she felt. Was it that she couldn't stand seeing a professor in his forties playing the fool in public, or was it the sight of his impenetrable innocence that she found impossible?

Everyone had laughed loudly. Hongmei had been silent. She had thought she must be bewitched by something. She'd never met a man like Glen, revealing so much of himself so quickly. After that, she had wanted to get close to him.

Words, when compared with feelings, are too concrete, too arbitrary, whereas feelings are richer but more elusive—ambiguous, if you will. Where words are muted, feelings begin.

— — —

She played Ping-Pong and tennis against him, fetched him alcohol from the infirmary when he needed it for a cheese fondue, led him on photo expeditions in *hutongs*, squeezed through the crowds of Xidan night market with him. She more or less forgot reality. Female classmates asked her presumptuously where she'd bought this or that new garment, and when she said it was secondhand, overseas discards from Xidan market, they exaggeratedly praised her powers of observation, clamoring for her to make another trip there, to pick up similar items for them too.

Once in the students' canteen Glen came in and joined several female students. He said the foreign instructors' cafeteria was out of food, and could they spare him a bite? The girls jostled to go stand in line a second time, returning with a dozen dishes for him. Then they noticed his eyes light up as he half rose from his bench. Turning around, they saw her walking in. All the while Professor Glen was bantering with them, he couldn't take his eyes off Hongmei. They abruptly realized that he was in the students' canteen to see her. Hoping to see a good show, they called her over to join them. She happened to be dressed simply that day, in a white blouse and olive-green trousers.

A short while later, Glen asked, "Did you get something on your sleeve?"

She replied, "It's ink. It was there before."

The other women didn't say a word, just listened to the pair of them talk. Glen wanted to know how the ink had gotten onto her sleeve. She said she'd done it herself. When she couldn't think of an answer in an exam, she'd drawn circles on her sleeve, ending up with a big blot. Glen said it could be washed off, and she said no, not possible; she'd tried everything. All eyes were on Professor Glen, then on Hongmei. There was something else going on here, but no one could tell what. Glen said, "You must be doing it wrong. Give it to me. I'll clean it for you." The women gasped, but Glen didn't seem to notice. "Let me have it, and I guarantee I'll hand it back tomorrow spotless."

Hongmei already had a sense of Glen's frankness, but even so, she didn't know how to respond. Her mouth was full, so she could only blush. Then she said the professor should change his line of work and open Glen's Laundromat.

He earnestly explained that he was used to doing housework. With fewer chores in China, he found he had too little with which to distract himself. He said, "If you don't believe me, just watch—I promise I'm not as bad as you think. I can definitely clean clothes like a pro."

The women departed soon after that, leaving Glen and Hongmei with a dozen dishes between them. There was an awkward silence, and she knew something was up.

This, she told the secret talker, had been a turning point in her relationship with Glen.

She more or less forgot that as a military interpreter, she was a first lieutenant, even though she mainly translated operating manuals. She couldn't go around so openly with a foreigner. But the worst part and the most worrying, she forgot she was supposed to be happily married. Every day she spent with Glen made her situation more and more dangerous. Staring at the tableful of food, she glanced at Glen. "What should we do now?" At the time, she'd had no idea this ambiguous, innuendo-laden question would create a secret space clearly separating inside from out, and place enormous pressure on both of them. They were now forced to quickly define the nature of this relationship, as well as what they were to each other.

Glen looked at her as if he were a child. "Did I say something wrong?"

"Do you really want to wash my blouse?"

"Really." He still had no idea what was wrong.

"You're hopeless," said Hongmei. She'd never felt so strange before. She had a sudden urge to stroke this overgrown child's head and tell him what was in her heart, though she shouldn't say the words out loud.

He must've felt close to her, deep down, and so displayed this intimacy in public for everyone to see.

"Can't I wash your clothes?" he asked.

"Do you do laundry for other female students?" she retorted.

"Depends on whom," he said.

"Who?" she pursued.

"I can't say. If I feel like doing it, then I will. Everyone makes me feel differently."

Hongmei tapped away at the keyboard, telling the secret talker that after that day, she understood what "ostracize" truly meant, a word Glen had taught her. The other students began ignoring her in class and in the cafeteria. Perhaps they were jealous, or she was getting too close to the foreigner. Yet Glen still invited her to read in class and praised the accuracy of her pronunciation, sometimes too much, more than a professor ought to compliment a student. For instance, he might say, "Wow, you have an exquisite voice." Glen openly gave in to his feelings, and she was the one who suffered for it. Every one of her classmates, male and female, thought she was shamelessly flinging herself at their tutor. Only several years later could she finally and openly admit to this person that she now understood she had indeed been pursuing her professor. From the very first class, she had spread a net for Glen. She couldn't be without a target; she was a woman who pursued men. She had also hunted down her first husband. She told the secret talker that she knew what sort of woman she was, a source of disaster, always causing trouble—at least that's how she saw herself. When in pursuit, she could be as fearless as a man, no matter the cost, no matter the consequences.

She added, The man I'm talking about is Glen, as he was then. Next I'll tell you how tragic his courtship was.

Take a breath, Hongmei told herself. *Who'd have thought what we actually caught was each other as we are today?*

You seem disppointed, the secret talker interrupted, misspelling the word again.

Yes, it did feel a bit like she'd been tricked. She wrote, Not long after I'd moved from my little village to the military academy in Nanjing, I experienced this faint disappointment. The world outside my little village wasn't as big as the educated youth had made it sound, nor even as big as I'd imagined. I wanted to see somewhere larger. I mean the unknown, like when Glen first showed up, and his every word and movement uncovered new ground. Even his smallest, most overlooked gesture. For instance, holding his sunglasses in his mouth while tying his shoelaces, or turning his baseball cap to the back when aiming a camera, picking up the napkin from his lap to wipe his mouth . . . It was after one of these gestures that I knew very clearly I'd fallen in love with him.

The person asked what the gesture had been. Hongmei felt a wash of warmth in her heart. When she first fell in love with Glen, these waves of tenderness often had overtaken her. Now they felt unfamiliar, as if she hadn't experienced them for many years. She wrote about this sensation, then described the evening Glen took her to Jianguo Hotel. This was about two weeks after her classmates had started giving her the cold shoulder. She no longer remembered if they'd had a big meal, but they probably had—back then Glen always ordered enough food for six. Then the bill came—Glen's lips didn't stop their stream of light conversation, nor did his eyes leave her face, but his right hand slipped into the left inner pocket of his suit and pulled out a black leather wallet. Moving casually, his second and third fingers fished out a credit card. The movement was infinitesimal and yet spoke of great generosity. He was still speaking to her, occasionally correcting her English grammar, then warmly apologizing. When the waitress came back with the receipt, he pulled a pen from his pocket and, with just a few wriggles of his wrist and an energetic tilt upward, he signed it. There it was, the living embodiment of someone from the wealthiest nation on Earth, a rich man who didn't care about money, giving her a new sense of cash with a flick of his pen. She pondered how rich a country would have to be to breed such nonchalance around money. She couldn't understand why that gesture had made Glen look so good, so American. They took the bus home. It was after eight, and the sky had just darkened. Glen's breath smelled faintly of wine, mixed with his after-dinner coffee. It was Sunday night, and the bus was crammed—everyone was rushing home. She and Glen stood facing each other, the alcohol swirling inside them. When the vehicle swerved violently, she took his hand. It was like the closing of a dam—in an instant, her drunkenness dissipated, swept away.

She told the secret talker that till this day she had been shocked at how reckless, desperate, and shameless she'd been. She hadn't even been thinking what future they had; only that she loved him in that moment. She wanted to conquer Glen, to possess him. She said Glen agreed, saying yes to her. His hand clasped hers back, tightly. Next, it slid up her naked arm. His fingers were icy cold, finally stopping at the collar of her dress, on her collarbone. Even if he'd touched the very center of her womanhood, he wouldn't have elicited such a strong reaction. Something murky happened inside her body, a vague tensing and relaxing. She said, Oh, you don't know how good it felt—like punishment, like pleasure.

— — —

Sitting in the library, Hongmei suddenly felt something odd. Swinging around, she found the boy at the next table staring directly at her, abandoning his online group chat. In his eyes, she was a woman scouring the net for love, cheeks flushed, eyes distracted. She logged off at once and walked briskly out of the library. The boy caught up with her at the entrance and asked if she wanted some weed, good-quality stuff. So *that* was the craving he'd suspected her of, and wanted to profit from.

Back at home, Hongmei got a call from her friend Shi

Nini saying she had some news. Nini was in the music department. Like Hongmei, she was getting degree after degree, living off scholarship grants. She was five or six years younger than Hongmei and often set her sights on some tycoon or another. As for her ultimate goal, she was very clear: if an average man was interested in her, she'd tell him not to bother—he couldn't afford her. She had a high-pitched voice, clear and sweet, the sort of unsexy, girlish way of speaking Americans detested. Now, though, it was suddenly deeper and breathier, as if blowing into Hongmei's ear.

"Guess what," she said. "I've nabbed a thirty-two-year-old millionaire."

"Well done," Hongmei replied.

Nini explained that the young millionaire owned a chain of high-end men's fashion stores. All the tycoons in Europe and America, in the whole world, bought his clothes. He had given Nini a job right away, as a manager at one of his branches. The young millionaire might have been on the cutting edge of fashion, but he liked long-haired Asian girls in jeans. As a result, according to Nini, her roomful of miniskirts that only covered half her ass were now on the scrap heap. She made a fuss about this, her voice rising again. "The last millionaire gave me a set of even, white teeth and paid for all my dental bills. Who knows—maybe this one will help fix my acne?"

Hongmei laughed. Nini didn't have many good points, but what stood out was her willingness to freely admit to selfishness, vulgarity, and an excessive fondness for money. Anyone who couldn't handle this knew to stay away or they'd get hurt. She knew she was a joke in many people's eyes, but she didn't care.

Hongmei said, "Nini, you've called at just the right time."

Nini immediately replied, "If you're asking for something, I'll hang up."

She ignored the jibe. "Nini, you have to help me with this."

"Don't you know me? I've never helped anyone before."

"You have to send an email for me, pretending to be all lonely and hurt."

"I am hurt," said Nini sarcastically. "I've cried myself to death. Go on, Qiao Hongmei, who do you want me to destroy?"

"Just a note saying you ran into him by chance somewhere and for some reason you want to talk to him again."

Hongmei gave her the email address and a rough outline of a message. This was a brainwave she'd had, to make her position in this roundelay less of a passive one. She was doing this on a whim. She wanted to see how he would react when ambushed by a female attacker. It was a test to see if he was interested solely in Hongmei or he just went for any Asian woman in a skirt. She wanted to make sure she was truly special in his eyes. Was it vanity? Either way, she couldn't help herself.

Nini responded after reading the email by asking if she should attach a photo, one in which her acne couldn't be seen. "Yes, how about a full-body shot!"

Hongmei disagreed. She thought Nini's photo was too sensual.

Nini yelped, "What about my alabaster tits and ass? Don't they count for something?"

Hongmei just laughed.

Nini asked, "Who is this?"

Hongmei replied, "A millionaire."

Nini said, "So if I nab this one, he's mine?"

"Yes, he's yours."

Nini phoned that night to say the millionaire was ignoring her.

She forwarded her email, and Hongmei read it twice and thought it sounded about right. She said to Nini, "Send another photo, this time with your hair down, wearing jeans."

After hanging up, she saw a new message ping in her inbox. It was the secret talker.

He said he was imagining what she might be doing. Midnight—is that wine or tea in your cup? Hongmei's hand closed tightly around her mug of tea.

He said he could see her in a voluminous housecoat, hair half tucked inside her collar. He said he liked her any way she looked. Beneath the baggy, soft fabric, her tiny naked body made him ache.

Hongmei suddenly felt warm all over.

He said that certain feelings, once you put them into words, weren't actually like that at all. This was his difficulty. What he wanted to transmit to her was sheer emotion, without the smug interpolation of words in between. Taste, breath, touch . . . How could words possibly describe these things? The sensation of licking a peeled grape can only exist between your tongue and the grape—the fullness of that lick, its translucent quality, so juicy and ripe, belonging only to the grape and not any other substance. He said even this was a distortion, him strong-arming the wordless meeting of tongue and grape, a secret between the two parties that only they could know. Words were too slow, too clumsy, too practical and solid, too stark and violent.

Her mouth grew moist, and something seemed to change inside her chest.

Imagine it, he said, your tongue encountering a perfect, perfect bit of cheese, or a drop of thirty-year-old red wine, or a most passionate pair of lips. None of these could be easily put into words. These secrets are almost sinful ecstasies for the senses. He said words disappointed him, the way they betrayed sensation. But he believed she understood what he meant, a secret between the two of them.

Just like the secret between the tongue and the grape, the wine, and the lips.

Without knowing how it happened, she logged off and walked into the bedroom. Glen was still reading his students' book reports on his laptop, looking peaceful in the lamplight. A clump of gray-white hair drooped over his temple, and his face was distinctly outlined. He hugged her and kissed her ear. This was all familiar, comfortable and numb. She didn't know why she took his hand and placed it on her breast. Glen made love to her the way he hadn't in a long time.

Afterward, he said, "Are you all right?" He sounded worried.

She was full of guilt. If Glen had said nothing, he wouldn't be Glen. How could she have sunk so low? Her body had run off, miles away.

She didn't sleep that night and got up at five in the morning to write the emailer a message. She thanked him for showing up and making the feelings she thought she'd lost come back again. He'd opened her up, body and soul. But this was going too far, and she was scared. She couldn't get hooked on this drug. She would be even more grateful if he could vanish.

After breakfast, she saw his reply, asking if she planned to change her email address.

She avoided the question and said she hoped this would

be the last message she'd get from him. He said that no matter what, he'd frequently watch her walk across the lawn. She said nothing but pressed down hard on the keyboard to exit the browser. She had a class that afternoon and picked up her books and notebook, returning to the living room. Glen had headed out at some point, leaving lunch for her—a convenience-store sandwich. She pulled back the plastic film and saw a pale pink slice of ham between two dark slices of bread, like a wound gaping open.

As Hongmei was walking across the lawn, she stopped. She looked all around, then turned her gaze back to the top of their sixteen-story building, the highest point on campus. A place where you could see everyone and everything.

Running up there, she found the door to the rooftop locked. She quickly found the super in the basement. Very politely, he asked what business she had on the roof. She said to look at the scenery. He said that wouldn't do; he wouldn't be able to explain that to the residents' board. She said she wasn't going to commit suicide, and he chuckled and said, "Who could possibly know that?" She said, "If you're worried, come up with me." His eyebrows lifted, to indicate that her invitation was charming and that he was receptive. Right away, it reverted to the sort of smile a fellow airline passenger shoots you to say they're done being social, and he said he didn't want to go look at the scenery.

Changing the subject, he thanked her for the books she'd donated to the communal laundry room—there was a shabby bookshelf there, and anyone was free to leave old books for others to read while waiting. People often took them home, replacing them with other books of their own, a virtuous circle. Hongmei asked how he knew she'd donated the books. He said because she'd donated so many books. She said they didn't have her name in them. He said, "Do they need to?" His eyes suddenly turned mysterious. Black eyes. Black hair. Five foot nine or so.

Hongmei thought she knew who the secret talker was. Her apartment building's super was as described in the earlier messages, and he knew the background, financial situation, and emotional state of every household.

The next day at noon, Hongmei saw the super walk across the lawn, sandwich in hand. She was seated on her balcony, wearing sunglasses. The super's ponytail blew in the wind, making him look for a moment like a melancholy drifter. *Look at that—I can fix you in my sights too.* The slight tilt of the balcony's sunshade made her position particularly ideal. *See, I can lurk in the shadows too, leaving you in the light.* The super sat down on a bench stippled with pigeon shit. It seemed he wanted to eat his lunch within Hongmei's line of sight. The two of them were now in the most clichéd scene of any thriller.

She casually swung her leg up, one foot resting on the

other knee. He hadn't unwrapped his sandwich. From sixteen floors up, he looked expectant. He was waiting for someone, constantly glancing at his watch. She looked at hers too: 12:59. Drug dealers usually showed up punctually, and his face was a little like an addict's.

A woman walked by: red hair, tall, and plump, like a good-hearted Irish mom who'd had a brood of kids. She was holding a sandwich too. This vast, diverse country had a massive population yet only a few varieties of food. A commonwealth united by fast food. The woman and the super both ate their sandwiches while looking at some sheets of paper. Soon afterward, their hands started moving, drumming out a beat on their legs. Hongmei stood up and leaned against the balcony railing.

Hongmei realized that they must be rehearsing a musical—perhaps they were a couple of amateur actors, playing bit parts for a local theater company. They sang energetically, the woman's chubby hand tapping against the super's back. The super seemed busy enough yet apparently still had time for secret meetings. She watched as they said goodbye, then hurried downstairs to the basement and met him coming out of the washroom. Seeing her, he staggered back a step or two. Hongmei felt a stab of pleasure—*See? I can take you by surprise too.*

Not missing a beat, he hinted that he had a bell.

She said, "Sorry. Pardon me. Your door was open."

He responded, "You want to look at the scenery again?" His laughter had even less restraint this time.

She said she'd locked herself out—could she use his computer?

Like a bit player in a musical, he extended a courtly invitation. She stared at him. Eyes, black; hair, black; ears, on the small side but exquisitely molded. She scanned his features and committed them to memory. He remained hidden behind whatever role he was playing in this musical and said theatrically, "Not at all. It's my honor to labor for an enchanting woman such as yourself." He seemed a little tense, though he kept up a flow of chatter. Next, he went over to a desk and pulled out a swivel chair for her. She shot him a look. So this was the man who wanted to confess his desires? There was some talent here, all that fine language blindly thrown away on her.

He asked if she wanted a glass of something.

She said, "Anything is fine. I'll drink whatever you have." A couple of clicks and the current started chirping through the space between him and her.

She took the water he handed her. This man who'd tricked her into trust and passion, secretly or openly running between all his many bit parts.

The new inbox was calm. Just a message from Nini. She opened it with a click, to see Nini had ended her five-day-old romance. She told Hongmei that an IT tycoon had come into her shop and bought tens of thousands of dollars' worth of suits. He'd asked her to come help him in the changing room, and they'd started making out right there. Nini had been ready to straddle two boats at once, but then she got her termination notice. It turned out the clothing tycoon had seen the whole thing through the shop's closed-circuit TV. Nini said, These days there's not one place where you'll be left alone! The super was now using a newspaper as camouflage. Hongmei wrote back to Nini. Then she sipped at the water in her glass.

Nini replied at once, saying she just got her first email from the secret talker. He had praised her youth and beauty, saying she was the sort of Asian woman every white man dreamed of. Nini didn't forward the whole message, keeping him for herself as she did the other tycoons.

6

Hongmei looked at the man hiding behind the newspaper. It kept rustling. *Don't think of getting rid of me. Weren't you longing for an intimate conversation?* Then her inbox lit up, and her scalp prickled. The secret talker! How was that possible? Hardly anyone knew her new email address.

He said right away that she oughtn't buy flowers from the cut-price stall—those petals were just glued on and would never bloom.

She asked if there was a need for him to follow her like that.

He said he was hooked on her, and that wasn't entirely his fault.

She said if that were really the case, he ought to come out from behind his computer or shrub or newspaper. Otherwise she'd consider her privacy invaded and call the police.

The newspaper shook again, urging her to go. A yawn,

a cough. Now that he was no longer under suspicion, he'd gone back to being a dull building super.

The secret talker said, Why do you have to treat me like this? A police report in exchange for my devotion?

She could see the tragic smile in his words. She answered: You make me feel like I have nowhere to hide. No, like there's nowhere I can be.

He apologized.

She said: If you won't go away, I'll get the police to lay an ambush. They'll be interested. Men kidnapping women and girls is a hot topic.

No response.

Five minutes later, a reply.

How can you be so sure I'm a man?

Hongmei stared at the words.

The super said, "You need any help?" He was finding all of this odd too. If she ever wound up screaming and cursing at someone in the street, she'd look no different from the way she did now. She felt vicious, coarse expressions exploding on her face one after another. She kept blowing aside the hair that fell across her face, her lips twitching nonstop. A female secret talker? In her mind, Hongmei kicked open this person's front door, grabbed their hair, and dragged them out into the street. She wasn't even sure if she was spelling some of these swear words correctly, but she didn't care When she paused and brought the glass to her lips, she found it empty. This person had toyed with her so much, she was half crazy. She slowly deleted her rant and coldly typed out, Then there's a fundamental misunderstanding between the two of us. I'm a straight woman—I only like men.

She logged off and stood up. The newspaper came down and revealed the super's knowing face. He'd seen her entire tirade, a flurry of furious typing. He'd just been playing the part of a meek little employee rather than sneakily trying to pair up with her. He bid her goodbye politely, saying he'd help her ask permission at the next residents' committee meeting.

She was confused—"Permission for what?"

He said, "To get the key to the roof, of course." What a good little employee, so responsible.

She said, "That's too much trouble. Forget it."

He said, "No trouble at all." Then, with a change of tone, "What on Earth are you planning to do up there?"

She asked what other residents went up for.

"Fixing TV antennae," he answered.

She said, "You see, if I'd said that's what I would be doing, wouldn't you have given me the key at once?"

He said, "That's right. You ought to have said that. I don't want to know what you would actually do up there."

She smiled. "I'm not going to kill myself."

He smiled too. "Can I trust you?"

She said, "Of course you can't."

He pulled a face at her, acknowledging her meaning. Just to be sure, she asked him how to spell "disappoint." He got it right, not a single letter missing. Her suspicions were completely dispelled now, and he was found not guilty.

— — —

The secret talker enlightened Hongmei, telling her there was no problem; it was safe to receive another woman's admiration.

Hongmei bluffed, I know who you are. When you're spying on other people, please don't forget that you're being spied on too.

This wasn't a complete lie. Not long after their first conversation about the secret talker, Nini had asked one of her male admirers to tail Hongmei in hopes of spotting the secret talker. On a couple of occasions, he'd spotted a tall, thin woman hanging around. She hadn't thought much about this clue, until now.

The secret talker said naturally she understood that she was definitely being spied on. She added, This has already become a tactic we mutually understand. Next, she continued with her solicitation, saying Hongmei ought to try loving a woman, because only another woman could take emotion as seriously as she did.

Hongmei said, Stop playing with me.

Five minutes later, she was back, saying, Weren't two marriages enough for you? Even with your current husband, don't you feel cheated? Why not try a woman? Otherwise you'll never know what you're missing.

Hongmei said, I'm going to make you reveal yourself.

The person was silent for a bit, then said, For the sake of a small clue, you've even missed your class—that wasn't worth it.

Hongmei thought, *So she even knows I skipped class*. On the keyboard, though, she teased, No matter what, I like your style. Your hair is great too, and your outfit. Everything is so nice, not at all like a Peeping Tom. Then she remembered something else Nini's spy had said: the tall woman had limped a little. She went on: Your way of walking is very bold, very distinctive. Why not just stand up straight and emerge from behind these beautiful words?

A long silence. Hongmei felt as if she and this other person were pugilists sparring in the dark, feeling their way, silently circling each other. Neither could afford a false move. Sure enough, the secret talker replied, asking Hongmei if she was treating everything she'd ever said as a joke. For instance, what about her long-lost daughter? She said that no matter what sort of demon Hongmei imagined she was, the daughter actually did exist. Like an unhealed wound, the daughter pained her from time to time.

In order to prove this, she sent a series of photographs. A girl growing from an infant to the age of ten, a sickly looking, sensitive child.

Hongmei was touched. This girl had the eyes of an old soul and looked heartbreakingly familiar. She examined the pictures carefully, one by one, trying to think whose eyes these were. She was almost certain she'd seen them before. As she stared, she realized with a start that another pair of eyes was watching her through the daughter's. Intuitively, she sensed that this person (whether a man or a woman) did have such a daughter, and that there had indeed been a tragedy with this child at its heart. She replied to say how pretty the girl was, though she had an air of misfortune. She said, I feel like I've seen those eyes somewhere before. No, it's not a feeling—I actually have.

The person answered that the reason she'd lost contact with her daughter for so many years was because of a single misdeed. During the divorce proceedings, she snatched the child from her school and hid her away for several months. At the time, it had felt like the only way she could keep her daughter, but they were discovered, and she lost custody.

Once again Hongmei could tell there was real anguish there even if this specific story didn't end up being real. Instinct told her this wasn't the extent of the suffering. She asked, Since your daughter went back home after this visit, has she called often?

The person said that in the end, her daughter hadn't completely believed her.

Hongmei asked, What do you want her to believe?

That I love her, that I'd never hurt her, no matter how many stupid things I've done, answered the person. Just as I don't want to hurt you. If you agree, I'll leave and never bother you again.

Since she'd stopped seeing this person as a "he," Hongmei now felt safer. When she was out walking, she would stop abruptly and look to see if the tall woman had shown up. Yet nothing was ever out of the ordinary. She had returned to her usual routine: going to the library, to school, to the mall, to the supermarket. This was much better; she no longer felt like she was in the path of a pair of beastly eyes. She realized she was staring at the secret talker's message, wondering which patch of shadow the woman had been hiding in to have seen her so clearly. She stereotypically imagined her to be like many of the other lesbians on campus: short hair, rimless glasses (or no glasses might be better?), defined features (but not a mask), and bottomless black eyes like the little girl's.

Feeling calmer, Hongmei told those black eyes what sort of person she was: a follower, too easily swayed by shallow sensual pleasures. More than a decade ago, for the sake of that first caress with Glen on the bus, she'd sacrificed everything, her job, her reputation, her marriage. The evening when four soldiers in full military dress escorted her from her classroom, she'd turned like the heroine of a tragedy and taken one long, last look at the light in Glen's hostel window.

That had been at the start of November, the coldest time in Beijing, a couple of weeks before the heating came on. Behind her were the twenty or so evening self-study classmates who'd watched as the soldiers had surrounded her. A military jeep was parked outside. She knew this was the vehicle that would take her away. She was mainly a translator of machine operation manuals but at that moment was accused of leaking Chinese military technology secrets. As absurd as the charge was, she had no choice but to comply. The jeep took her to a patch of wasteland. What would Glen do? Wait for her at the "usual place"? Or would he give up and start wandering around, searching for her? Soon, her classmates would tell Professor Glen where the girl called Qiao Hongmei had gone—a place she'd never come back from; a few rows of simple huts in the wilderness, one of which had been turned into a temporary cell.

The soldiers brought her into a large room filled with piercing light. Waiting there were three officers, one deputy regiment commander and two company commanders. The interrogation began. She sat in the position of the accused, her icy hands clenched into fists. They asked what she thought of Professor Glen. She said: "Scholarly, upright." They said, "When he passed on the secret reports you gave him, he only used one word to describe you: 'unique.'" She said she'd never passed on any so-called secret reports. They told her Professor Glen's letters home to America had been decoded, and they contained huge amounts of classified information. She said that was impossible. She spoke a great deal, trying to make them grasp a simple fact: from the start of her job to the present moment, she'd not been in contact with a single document containing the word "classified." Besides, her main task was to translate English instruction guides into Chinese, so what secrets could she possibly pass on? The questioning went on for weeks. She became severely sleep deprived and lost her appetite. But the greatest torment was not having fresh underwear to change into. She knew they intended not just to punish but also to humiliate her.

They were deadlocked, tossing the same few questions and answers back and forth, until suddenly, at the three-week mark, the interrogation stopped and she was told to write out her every encounter with Glen, every word, every action, every detail, to record all of it with dates.

Hongmei told the secret talker that she'd handwritten more than three hundred pages of this "regret journal" when she had a sudden revelation about herself. She now knew herself to be a woman for whom monogamy was difficult. Each time she met a new man she would forget everything else and go after him. "New" as in someone who had a mystique about them and gave her a sense of the unknown, snapping short her destiny with her existing man. She said that as a girl from a small village, she was attracted to distance, to anything or anyone that felt foreign. When Glen had said "I love you" in class with that bizarre pronunciation, she had become obsessed. Those three Chinese words, spoken by him, had seemed to transcend themselves, a breakthrough in linguistic expression.

She said, Glen, this American man more than twenty years older than me, smashed the world as I knew it and opened up a vast swathe of unknowing. While I was there, every glance, every touch, felt wonderful. When our last line of defense falls, I think I could die there.

Perhaps the consciousness of those two hundred thirteen young girls now resided in her. A shame they would never know what they were missing out on.

The secret talker responded, asking how she had gotten back together with Glen.

After a forced confession, Hongmei was released from prison. It took two years of her working in various humble jobs before she was finally able to squeeze a little extra money out of her salary after paying her rent and meals. One day as she walked past a public phone booth, she stopped. Yes, two years had passed. And Glen was then a

Pacific Ocean away from her. Yet the love and longing for him still hurt so much. She found herself on the street, asking to change a ten-yuan bill for coins. She walked back to the phone booth and started inserting coins. She pulled out a business card that Glen had given her, on which he'd written out the spelling of the word "ostracize."

She made that transpacific phone call to Glen's office. This was the only piece of information she had about him. She got his voicemail, asking her to leave a message. She said, "Hi Glen . . ." but couldn't go on. How many times could he have stopped loving her, found someone else, in those two years? She'd lost her rank, her urban residency permit, her husband, and her home, ending up as a temporary worker in a small private business. She'd planned to say, "Glen, I love you"—two years ago, the two of them hadn't bothered and so had missed out on saying the words that would have clarified their status. But she couldn't make herself do it—those words weren't as full of meaning as "Hi."

7

Three days after that, Glen showed up at her office in a track-suit and a baseball cap. If he hadn't been carrying a travel bag with the United Airlines logo, she would have thought he'd come straight from a long jog.

The secret talker said, Very good—a fairy tale ending.

Hongmei responded, If this were the ending, it really would be a very sweet fairy tale.

She shut down the computer and thought moodily, *What is wrong with me? Treating this person like a confessor, or a shrink? Isn't this in a way also masturbatory?*

— — —

Nini called to her from the classroom door, "Hongmei, problem!" Her arms were waving wildly over her head, revealing freshly shaved armpits. "The secret talker wrote again last night!"

Hongmei told her to speak Chinese, and while she was at it to cut down on the histrionics.

Nini told her the secret talker was actually a twenty-year-old woman! The night before, she'd messaged Nini late into the night, saying she'd caused someone's death. Her long fingers dug into Hongmei's forearm. "I asked her whose death. She only explained herself in the small hours of morning."

Here's what happened. At the age of six, this self-proclaimed woman of twenty had been undergoing hypnosis therapy for her anxiety when she mentioned incest during a session. Over the next two years, the therapist used the clues she provided while in a trance to deduce and finally solve the case, working out that between the ages of five and six the girl had been repeatedly raped by her father. She'd completely forgotten this traumatic episode, but hypnosis had brought the memories back. This coupled with her parents' messy divorce was enough evidence to bring the father to court, where he was almost bankrupted by the legal fees, and his reputation was destroyed. The therapist went on to write a bestselling book about the affair, turning their trauma, fake or real, into gold. With his final words, written before his suicide, the father wanted the girl to understand that he would die bearing a grudge—he and she were both victims of persecution. As an adult, the girl gradually came to understand that her father might truly have been innocent, that it was the therapist who'd induced her, while she was little, to say what she did—maybe for fame or chasing a Freudian theory—so her words could then be further twisted into testimony against her father. The outcome had been terrible. Now all grown up, she believed it was impossible to completely forget such a harrowing event. No matter what Freud might have hypothesized about humanity's ability to repress memory, the fact that she didn't remember these rapes could only mean they never happened in the first place.

Hongmei read through Nini's email printouts, her eyes lingering on the final paragraph: "This will be my last message to you. I know I've disppointed you, because you weren't looking for a girlfriend like me." The same misspelling.

She asked Nini if she really believed the secret talker was a twenty-year-old girl.

Nini said she was utterly confused and had no idea what she did or didn't believe.

They were at the campus sports field. Half the townspeople had congregated here, watching some radical students get ready to burn the flag. The protests in San Francisco, a two-hour drive away, had been going on for two months now, though this was the first major activity at the university. One student was reading Martin Luther King Jr.'s "I Have a Dream" speech over a loudspeaker while others climbed the pole and brought down the flag. As with most other places in America, sixty-five percent of the people in this town were fat. A visual reminder of their wealth, their excess—something Hongmei hadn't understood until she moved here. The overweight populace was raising a cheer when the police arrived. At the same time, the flames started.

Police cars surrounded the crowd. An obese police officer waved at people he recognized. The students led a chorus of "Give Peace a Chance."

Hongmei wondered where the secret talker was at this moment.

Back at the condo, she found no one on the lawn—everyone was watching the excitement. It was noon and so quiet she could hear her skirt rustling against her legs. Glancing at her watch, she noticed one of the elevators had been on the sixteenth floor for five minutes now. The other one had an OUT OF ORDER sign. All the residents must be watching the flag-burning from the roof. Not much happened in this town.

She decided to climb the stairs. On the seventh floor, she realized there was another set of footsteps, also heading up. She started stomping, ascending a few more levels, and the other person did so too, as if in response, the echoes taking a while to fade. She felt something prickle on her back—beads of sweat like countless little bugs wriggling from their eggs, poking their heads out, then crawling all over her. She tried to calm down. What was there to be afraid of, in broad daylight? Yet she'd never seen such a deserted day. She decided to tiptoe down and catch her chaser, but the other person retreated even faster. She thought, *How come now I'm the pursuer?* Rapidly, she drew closer to the other person. Now she was chasing full throttle, but the other pair of feet were nimble too, vaulting away in a series of dancing leaps. At the ground floor, there was nowhere to go. The foyer was more than a thousand square feet and empty, containing nothing but three armchairs for visitors.

Hongmei hadn't expected him (or her) to scurry down to the underground parking garage. She wasn't going to follow. What if it was a trap? Countless horror movies had shown her that parking garages were the perfect places to get murdered.

She trudged back up, heading to her apartment in defeat, legs trembling violently. At the fourth floor, she heard the metal garage door clang. He (or she) was back again. Another pair of exhausted legs, dragging him (or her) upward. She crept up, and he (or she) slowly followed.

Hongmei sat down on the steps at the ninth floor. Even the most fancy apartment buildings had dark stairwells with no windows, illuminated only by energy-saving lights, the permanent grayish glow spilling onto bare concrete steps. After a minute, she was about to stand when she caught a whiff of weed. A respectable resident of this building forced into this nasty place to satisfy a craving. Those footsteps hadn't been following her at all; it was just some addict trying to avoid trouble.

— — —

Glen wasn't home. He'd left a note saying he was off to watch the flag-burning. He'd scrawled these words—so the chaos was affecting him too. These last few years, she and Glen had been communicating more and more through notes. It saved time, and they were less likely to quarrel.

Turning on the computer, a glass of wine in hand, she prepared to have a proper chat with the secret talker.

She told her the story of the girl who'd destroyed her father. Perhaps the secret talker was familiar with this tale? But by the end of the tale, Hongmei's tears were flowing down her cheeks. After leaving his suicide note, the father had driven into the New Mexico desert and overdosed on sleeping pills. He hadn't wanted his daughter to see his corpse.

The next day, the secret talker still hadn't replied. Glen was bustling in and out, posting bail for students from his department who'd been arrested. Several others wanted to enlist, and he was talking to the university to guarantee their readmission. Hongmei found this Glen, with three days' worth of stubble on his face, much more alluring, as if she were having a brand-new crush on him.

Day three—still no response from the secret talker.

Hongmei sat before the computer, her mood gray.

Maybe telling her over and over that she liked men had led to this abandonment. Or maybe she'd thought that Hongmei and Nini were in cahoots to play a trick on her. Then it was seven days without a message. Hongmei stared at the blank screen and felt herself drawn into the twists and turns of this mazelike secret talker. Her desk was a jumble—two mugs, the coffee in them solidified; a sandwich on the computer, one bite taken out of it, the protruding ham dried out to the deep red of an old wound. Behind her, the study was a wasteland too, six or seven books lying open beneath a layer of dust. Her mirror was covered in little notes, reminding her to take back her library books, to return Professor So-and-So's call, to water the plants. The one hanging from the window hadn't died of thirst yet but seemed to thrive in its unkempt state, even as a spider spun a web from it up to the ceiling.

The email finally came on the eighth day, resolutely refusing to mention Hongmei's last message about the girl who had ruined her father. She said that when Hongmei had walked down the long supermarket aisle, she almost hadn't noticed her. Dressed in white shorts and a red tank top, Hongmei had looked tall and limber, her every movement full of life. She had looked like an officer from the People's Liberation Army, someone you'd be careful not to provoke. The secret talker had looked at this former lieutenant's profile for a couple of minutes, trying to adjust her mystical, wafting image.

Compared to your husband, you're much more vigorous. Your hairstyle was surprising too—you're a woman of many transformations.

She'd watched Hongmei leave Glen's side, turning back to read a flyer on the floor. It was for subletting a house, the cheap rent scrawled across the front in Sharpie, circled in scarlet. Hongmei's white tennis shoe had landed on the flyer and twisted it so the words faced her, then she'd reached for a bottle of peanut oil, revealing the BCG vaccine scar on her arm. The secret talker said this scar had made her feel confused. Or let's be honest: it had filled her with desire.

Sounding unashamed, the secret talker revealed that she'd stood there for a long time, trying to hide her useless appearance.

She watched Glen's arm go around Hongmei's body, his fingers sliding numbly across the scar. She imagined Hongmei at age six or seven, standing among the other children, one sleeve rolled up. The secret talker had followed behind Hongmei, watching Glen with his arm still around her walking toward a food sample stand. She thought of a village girl at the age of seven, her hair pulled into thin pigtails as dry as withered grass, slowly moving her bare little feet to keep up with the rest of the kids, her face as unknowing as those around her, ready for the slaughter. She said she'd had a strong emotional response, wanting to touch that scar— from childhood to adulthood, the only thing that didn't change, preserving its unusual sensitivity.

She said she was sure Hongmei had actually memorized the price mentioned on the flyer. She'd stumbled upon a secret longing.

Or maybe in that instant you had a sudden urge to have a nest of your own. Who knows? No one can ever be fully aware of how many plans are sprouting in the darkness at the bottom of their heart. Then some outside event suddenly happens, abruptly illuminating those pitch-dark schemes. As for exactly what it is—separation, divorce, or an affair—you aren't sure. But the scheme has a beginning. Then you walked back to your husband, nestling against him like a baby bird.

She said at the sample counter Glen had been joking loudly. Like many Americans, he often used humor to alleviate the pressure that silence brings, averting a conversational crisis. Hongmei had laughed, but it had been apparent that inside it was all Hongmei could do to endure this. Even she had seen it, the cold reprimand in Hongmei's mouth.

Your intimacy makes me anxious, but you did well,

successfully putting up with that discordant joke. Then you watched your husband pick up a second piece of pastry, and it felt like you'd never noticed before that his entire scalp moves when he chews. There he was, mouth working away, picking up a third piece for you. You smiled and declined. He let out a satisfied sigh, and you turned your face aside to avoid that burst of hot, sweet breath. You looked around you. Fat bodies pushing overweight carts, double chins and huge red faces. So much food, enough to drown these fortunate people. Yet it all tastes alarmingly bland. These plump chickens—it only takes them as little as a month to go from hatching to becoming a pile of meat, no longer than the life span of a mushroom, and tasting about the same. You rummaged around the chicken shelf, looking for a half dozen leaner drumsticks, but you failed. In their short, untroubled lives, these chickens' feet never touch the ground, so their legs can grow till they reach a planned weight. Rows and stacks of plump bodies like in a group exercise class, whether male or female, weak or strong, their minds completely blank. How could they possibly taste of anything? The battle for survival, the urge to find a mate, the fear of natural enemies, the circulating blood and burgeoning flesh—all of that forms, fills each chicken's life with possibilities. It's precisely these possibilities that make a chicken what it is, rather than a mushroom. Finally, you picked up a pack of breast meat, because it was fifty percent off. You put it in the shopping cart, or rather tossed it in. I saw all the weariness, discontent, and helplessness in that moment. Your body language might be restrained, but it's never monotonous.

Hongmei heard Glen making a call in the living room, his voice sounding youthful. He was discussing the candlelight vigil taking place in San Francisco's Union Square the following night. More than two thousand people had registered online. Soon after that, she heard his excited footsteps charging over, pausing outside her door for two seconds, and then hurrying on to his own study.

She heard him get online, his fingers tapping smoothly away at the keyboard.

She read the secret talker's email three times, all the while running through the faces she'd seen that day in the supermarket. She'd let this person get away again.

She asked her to please stop playing this spying game.

The reply came right away, asking if she was really interested in subletting that cheap house.

Hongmei felt a wave of revulsion and banged out the words: My husband's next door, I could ask him how to deal with a pervert like you. He's already suspicious because of my strange behavior recently.

That can't be. From my observation, your husband believes you've entered into a period of absolute stability in your marriage. So stable you don't even need to share what's in your hearts. Not even those meaningful glances—those were gone long ago. Like most Americans, you fill the silence with chitchat and laughter, killing off the countless possibilities that lurk within quietness. Isn't silence its own form of understanding? Be boldly silent, and understanding will grow. Your husband's already lost the courage to say nothing. How many people lose this courage? Soon you will too.

The secret talker was growing cryptic, even mysterious.

8

Hongmei talked about the weeks leading to her departure from Beijing. A storm had swept over the city, and like the prince in "Cinderella," Professor Glen had found his bride. He returned to America before her but made sure to mail money for a plane ticket and two beautiful dresses. Half a year and mountains of paperwork later, she was preparing to leave the country.

It was early November, a night not too different from the night of her interrogation two years previously. She cycled back to the courtyard she'd once left each day to go to work, where she'd engaged in political study, taken part in the spring-cleaning, and distributed New Year's goods. A classic Beijing northern wind was blowing, catching fallen leaves and garbage. She knew her ex-husband had a girlfriend. She'd said to him on the phone, "Congratulations on finding a good woman, Jianjun." That was when he'd told her to come fetch her clothes and books.

Now she told the secret talker that after that phone call, the guilt she felt toward Jianjun stopped rearing up. He was very calm, telling her to bring someone to help when she came for her things, as it might be hard for a lone woman to run up and down the stairs so much—hinting that he wouldn't be lending a hand. He also told her that his girl-friend would be there.

She rode past the canteen, bathrooms, and convenience store, and then abruptly remembered that the latter made their own ice creams in the summer. These melted easily because they contained a lot of milk. Jianjun would buy a dozen at a time, tying them together with a hankie, then would sprint the hundred yards to her sixth-floor office. They'd be half melted by the time he got there, and Jian-jun would be too, smiling as he dripped with sweat. Next was a clinic, the light in the shift room as dim and grubby as it had been two years ago. The ambulance driver was still playing cards with Old Wang from the boiler room.

She locked up her bike and went into the clinic, where she made a phone call. She heard the person who answered shouting two stories above her. After a while, she heard a door open. The door to what used to be her home. She heard Jianjun's footsteps coming down the stairs to the phone and could tell he was still wearing the fake leather slippers she'd given him. He said, "Hello, who is this?"

She said nothing. He could already hear it.

Five minutes later, he had entered the clinic. He'd changed into an almost-new shirt, and his hair was styled the way she liked it. He said, "Let's go." Not even thinking about it, she followed him out the clinic's front door and up the stairs. Along the way, he asked her when she was leaving for America and if her parents were coming to see her off. She answered his questions one by one. As for the hurt and humiliation she'd brought him, she pretended it had nothing to do with her; as for the revenge and punishment he owed her, he'd let it go.

His girlfriend wasn't home. Hongmei didn't ask why, and he didn't explain. She noticed the set of imported furniture she'd chosen had finally arrived—three years from ordering to delivery. The pale yellow couch with a print that made it look embossed, the four-door wardrobe—a break from the uniformity of local products—the stainless-steel desk lamp. Even the dust cover for the TV set was exactly what she had wanted. While she'd been mired in detention, unemployment, and homelessness, the home she'd designed had been completed as planned. Everything was good, so good it felt like a scam. She thought grimly that Jianjun had enlarged and completed the trap she'd set for him.

He asked if she'd eaten and, without waiting for a reply,

went into the kitchen and turned on the stove. He said it was only canteen food, but luckily they had been serving her favorite lion's head meatballs. They sat at the small table. He kept her company as she ate, not saying much but touching on all the painful or sensitive points. There was laughter, and also tears. So Jianjun could be this gentle too, no longer the imposing, coarsely bellowing, mid-ranking army officer.

They talked about when they first met. He had been president of their senior class. He'd sent her love notes back to her but secretly bought her a pair of gloves and a set of *Lu Xun: Selected Works* in English translation. He admitted that he had wanted to possess her. When they went out together, if their hands happened to touch, it had felt like torture. She asked if he remembered their first time. He blushed and said, "How could I not remember? Didn't you write it all out in your self-criticism?"

At the time, he'd challenged everyone, "Punish me. I was the one who seduced her." They said nothing more, just exchanged a deep smile.

It wasn't clear who began it, but then they were hugging. Perhaps she was the instigator. She told the secret talker, It felt like I was the only guilty party. Jianjun carried her into the bedroom but seemed to lose his strength as he shut the door. She had her back to the door, and he was already kissing her. His lips had a trace of distant smoke.

He felt so much younger as he kissed her eyebrows, her eyes, her lips. She returned this with ten times the frenzy. He reached out and traced her features, across her brows and down to her nose, along the bridge and slowly farther down, outlining her lips, stopping on her lower one, the moist inside, sketching it over and over. This provocative, seductive, maybe even destructive finger, made her whole body clench. It was Jianjun's finger. She felt like she'd found something she'd lost. Jianjun continued his tracing, his finger going everywhere, a line of sparks along her skin. There were tears in his eyes, and hers too. He didn't recognize this woman's body—another man's incursion had made it unfamiliar and mysterious again. How could it take pleasure in the embrace of a foreign man? Jianjun couldn't imagine it. The earliest jealousy and rage had passed, and now he just found the whole affair inconceivable.

She'd never expected it would end up this way. They were making this perfect. So it turned out Jianjun could be this sensitive, this responsive to her needs. Tears covered her face, and she asked herself, *Why did you leave him? So you still have feelings for Jianjun. So you still love him.*

They lay in the same positions as before. His tears plopped onto her forehead, while hers dampened the hollows of his collarbones and shoulders. After a bout of weeping, they grew passionate again. In the small hours of the night, they grew exhausted. At dawn, she said she should be going. Then she said she wasn't leaving, she would never leave. She said, "Jianjun, if I stayed, if I didn't go, would you be happy?"

He sighed heavily and asked why she wouldn't go.

She said, "Because I've only just understood you. Isn't that terrible, Jianjun? I had to make such an awful mess and hurt us both so badly before I could understand you."

Jianjun asked what she understood. She said she understood how loving he could be. He laughed bitterly and said hadn't he always been like this?

She said, "No, not like this." He'd never spoken to her the way he had this night, nor had he ever looked at her this way, though how would he know that—he couldn't see his own expression. Then she added that he'd never kissed her and caressed her the way he had this day. She knew he might misunderstand, might think she was trying to shrug off responsibility.

He held her tighter, until she was gone. She wondered what kind of wretch she was. When newly engaged to Glen, her passion for her ex-husband had flared. Could she only find satisfaction within the wreckage of a ruined relationship? Why was it only at this moment she saw clearly that she'd never stopped loving Jianjun? One man wasn't enough for her, would never be enough. She'd always need to weave tangled, complex webs of emotion, jumbling the respectable and the unseemly, the open and the secret. Jianjun had swapped places with Glen, becoming the lover to be occasionally enjoyed. This thought alone was bizarre enough to set all her senses tingling. The feeling was amazing, flowing smoothly to the tip of every hair.

She started pulling on her clothes. Jianjun got up to help her with the zipper on her sweater. She turned back to look at him, tears flowing. This Jianjun was no longer the Jianjun of the past but a lover she'd newly acquired, one she loved madly but would shortly have to leave. She felt as if her mind was divided into several secret compartments, storing various types of love or emotion, and she had to distribute them among different men.

She wasn't a good woman, Hongmei frankly admitted to the secret talker. She was holding a bright red cosmopolitan, a cherry stuck on the thin rim of her glass. She'd mixed it herself, changing the proportions so this one had more vodka than usual. As she read through the message she'd just finished writing, she found that the late hour and the alcohol had made her honest. Before her was a gentle soul. Whether male or female, they were kind, not easily offended, and kept their feelings to themselves, like all great priests or psychiatrists. She could pour her heart out to this unseen figure and feel she wouldn't be judged, only accepted. For a moment, she forgot that she was the one repenting, and the person accepting her repentance was the secret talker in the depths of the computer. Only she felt that the two of them got on well, one standing, one kneeling. Whatever roles human beings played by day, if they didn't have a moment like this when they could reveal themselves, they'd surely be driven mad.

She continued unburdening herself. All those years ago, a week before leaving China, she hid herself in her new lover's chamber. This new lover was the husband she'd abandoned. For two days she stopped making love to him, just clung to him tightly from nightfall till dawn. Without transgression, happiness wasn't real. She then carefully put aside her passionate romance with Jianjun. When she got off the plane, walking into the dazzling California sunshine and Glen's embrace, her smile was a little crooked. She told Glen how much she loved him, and that was the truth—it felt as if her unfaithfulness had made her love him even more. Every woman finds that a secret passion increases her ardor and warmth for her husband, and every lucky husband should thank his shadowy rival, whether real or imagined. The security of a household stems from feelings constantly going their own way, conscience and falsehood adjusting each other, the third point of a triangle forever shrouded in darkness.

Finishing her drink, Hongmei found herself in an excellent state of drunkenness.

She told the secret talker there were moments when she'd discover with a shock how much she didn't love Glen. These often had happened when she had been living with Jianjun too. That's when she'd most longed for an affair.

9

At half past one in the morning, she shut down her computer and lurched into the bathroom to wash up. As she picked up her toothbrush, she suddenly felt she needed a bath. She had to own up to it, the shame and filth she felt within herself. Yet she had a pure heart too. Looking at the wavering lines in the mirror, she thought she was still beautiful and could be forgiven a little indiscretion.

In the morning, Glen insisted on dragging her to the square to see the university's new flagpole gadget. A little black box, halfway up. If anyone tried to bring the flag down, the box would turn into a vacuum and suck up the fabric. This was meant to deter anyone thinking of burning the Stars and Stripes.

Two people were up a ladder testing this device—just like magic, the waving flag got pulled into the little box, and the spectators clapped and cheered. A sea of pinkish faces beneath the blue sky, unblinking eyes—blue, gray, brown, black . . .

"Isn't this great?" Glen, thinking it was a nice invention, asked Hongmei.

Her palms were tapping together too. She nodded at Glen, wondering which pair of eyes belonged to her, the secret talker, who managed to be everywhere at once.

"A college in the Midwest came up with this," said Glen. "Never mind that we're in the red, the administration bought three right away."

She reached out to hug Glen. These were the moments she loved him most, his childlike enthusiasm.

Nini squeezed her way over to them, followed by two of her students aged fifty or sixty that she taught Chinese folk music to—this was her side job. She told Hongmei in Chinese that the secret talker was getting upset and had said that if Nini didn't stop harassing her, she'd get someone to deal with her. Nini saw Glen looking inquisitively at her and trotted out the expression she usually used to torment him—a lifted chin, rolled eyes.

As Nini began to leave with her overage students, she turned back to Glen. "You're very naughty. You didn't give me a dirty phone call last night!" To Glen's blank stare, she laughed. "Look at him, useless! Doesn't even know how to enjoy a joke!"

Hongmei cried out suddenly, "Nini, have you found a new apartment?"

"Still searching," she called back.

Each time an affair ended, she had to change her address. Hongmei said she knew a good place with cheap rent. Nini wanted to know if she could have pets. Hongmei said to call and ask for herself, then blurted out the phone number. Before she'd finished speaking, she had the thought that she had indeed been secretly longing for a private nest and had been thinking of running away. That's why she'd quietly remembered the number on the flyer. She glanced sideways at Glen. The five o'clock sun tinted his eyelashes gold, making them look extra long, flicking up more than usual. Now he had a child's eyes. She thought, *How on Earth could he know what this woman next to him was planning all day long?* Then she thought, *This woman noticed a housing ad and wants to leave him, but for whom? No, for what?* Was she running into the unknown?

— — —

The reply had been sent the night before, the night Hongmei had been tipsy. The secret talker told her that she happened to know the layout of Hongmei's apartment: bedroom, two studies, living room, bathroom . . . 2,000 square feet, a standard middle-class dwelling. (No need to be mysterious about it; there were floor plans at the Realtor's office—you only had to go in and pretend you wanted to rent a place.)

She told Hongmei that the previous midnight she'd stood outside the building. Her eyes had climbed floor after floor until they reached the southeast-facing window on the sixteenth floor. She had been certain that the figure seated beside this brightly lit square was Hongmei. Sitting down on a bench, the secret talker had taken a small bottle of Courvoisier from her pocket.

At this point, Hongmei's chair squeaked and she felt a shiver pass through her. She'd been drinking too at that moment!

That was her study—from the quality of the light, it was probably a drafting lamp. Right? she asked. She said she'd never realized how good alcohol could taste, when enjoyed on a lawn in the middle of the night. Facing Hongmei's window, she had drunk slowly, now and then raising the bottle in an unrequited toast to the woman upstairs.

Hongmei found this wraithlike woman terrifying. She pulled her legs up onto the chair and found her toes cold and white. No wonder the urge to unburden herself had been so strong last night—she must have sensed this. That bottle hadn't been raised in vain, the amber Courvoisier along with her deep red cosmopolitan. The secret talker said her addictions of twenty years ago were under control now.

The security guard's patrol cart had passed by her once every ten minutes, slowing down as it did so, then speeding up again. Soon, it was every eight minutes, and then every five. The guard had been afraid she would murder someone, or get murdered herself.

Then the light in the window went out, and she drank her last mouthful of cognac. She got up from the bench and went around to the back of the building, the security guard following in his cart.

On the other side, she saw another window lit up, long and narrow—the bathroom. She had stopped there.

Hongmei felt another tremor. That's when she'd been looking sensually at herself in the mirror. No wonder she'd felt so strange—another pair of eyes had been staring through hers. Possessed by a strange body, which used her gaze to stare at her drunken flesh, watching as her private self emerged from the shadows. A strange body!

Downstairs, the watcher had tilted her face up. The light in the narrow window had stayed on a full half hour. That's when scalding water had poured over Hongmei's head. In the lamplight, the water had turned into glittering crystals on her narrow shoulders and the slight protrusions of her breasts. It had felt good because of the little shock it imparted when it touched the skin. The secret talker told Hongmei that even the greatest comfort on Earth contained discomfort within it, and there was always a moment of surprise from the senses. She said in that half hour Hongmei had been in this state of shock, every strand of hair fully alive, her muscles swelling, the round scar on her arm as red and itchy as when she was seven.

Hongmei hated her in this moment, the secret talker. Just as she used to suddenly find herself loathing Jianjun. She could also turn Glen into a temporary enemy.

She wrote back immediately, saying, Enough! Stop exercising this obsession with me. She said, I'm not prey for seducers like you. I'd never have a fling with another woman.

The response: Don't be so sure.

Hongmei said the secret talker left her mentally and physically exhausted, so she often dozed off in class, yet she stayed awake all night long. This was the last stage of her PhD, and she was already on the brink of collapse.

Sure enough, this appeal to pity yielded results. The woman apologized and said, In that case, I'll love you from a distance. If you feel stifled or despairing, just come outside and you'll sense me. Your elegance will never flow away in vain; I'm the reason you're beautiful.

Afraid of getting stung again by pretty words, Hongmei quickly logged off and created yet another new email address, which she told only seven people about, asking them to keep it a secret. If she got any more messages from the secret talker, suspicion would fall on this group.

Next, she printed out every email she'd ever received

from the secret talker and read them one more time. "Disp-pointment" or its variants appeared eighteen times, and four more in Nini's messages. Twenty-two in total, missing the same letter each time.

She had several days of peace, during which her inbox remained empty. On day five, she got a message from Jianjun, just a few lines, saying his wife had had a baby.

After Hongmei had left Jianjun, her hysterical love and desire for him had subsided, and with his marriage, promotion, and renovation of the three-bedroom apartment he'd been newly allocated, it had evaporated altogether, like the new liaisons she kept seeking out. Just some encounters based on tacit understandings, ambiguous smiles, hugs and kisses disguised as politeness. These were mostly shared with Glen's colleagues or friends, those possessing their own homes and dishonest hearts. Their enchantment with her was based on a misreading, and she tried to maintain these beautiful misunderstandings as long as possible.

Back to her regular life with Glen. The scary part was over, and they could treat the stillness and monotony as peace and try to enjoy it that way.

— — —

Nini showed up uninvited, speaking loudly in Chinese as soon as she came in. Nini was taking a break from love, and her current boyfriend was just someone to go sight-seeing with. So she had a lot of free time to dedicate herself to the mystery of the secret talker. She'd found a girl in her twenties in San Francisco, she said, who looked exactly like the one in the photo. Hongmei asked, "What photo?" and Nini switched to English: "The father killer!" Glen, forking a piece of grilled fish just then, heard this explosive word and let the fish fall back onto the plate. He stared at the two Chinese women, trying to understand.

Nini said, "I'm describing a horror film." She knew Glen wouldn't believe her, but he also didn't know how to deal with her.

She told Hongmei that in the photos the twenty-something woman had emailed Hongmei, one was a close-up, with a backdrop of an archway wreathed in vermilion bougainvillea, the top of a fire tower visible on the left. Going by the angle of the photo, she'd located the archway. She had the address if Hongmei wanted to see for herself. Hongmei declined for now. She wasn't ready to confront the secret talker. Not yet. Nini and her boyfriend had sat at the coffee shop opposite and waited. Around six in the evening, the woman finally showed up. She was driving an old, white Toyota, wearing DKNY sunglasses, Calvin Klein jeans, and Nine West leather sandals. Her toenails were unpolished, and a dozen silver bracelets jangled round her wrist as she walked. There didn't seem to be anything wrong with her at all—she certainly didn't look parricidal. She had said this last word in English.

"A hundred-dollar word!" Glen exclaimed.

Nini said, "Haven't you noticed I love using big words?"

Hongmei said calmly, in Chinese, "You use Chinese to talk nonsense, then switch to English for the important words—place names, coffee shops. Careful." She then asked, "Did you talk to her?"

"Around seven o'clock I rang her bell. She opened the door, barefoot, still chewing. I asked if she recognized me. She stared at me for a while and shook her head with a confused smile. I could tell right away she wasn't bluffing—she really didn't know who I was. Which meant she hadn't seen all those photographs I'd emailed."

As she spoke, Nini got herself a glass and poured herself a little white wine. "She asked how I knew her. I couldn't answer, so she said it must be online; a lot of magazines have published articles about her. I didn't even know her name, but now I couldn't ask—that would give the game away. I said yes, I'd learned about her story online. She said she was sorry she couldn't ask me in. I knew she was trying to get rid of me, so I quickly left."

Hongmei couldn't work out what kind of spell this had been.

Nini was enthusiastic enough to offer up her boyfriend as a sacrifice. She dismissed guys like him as pretty but useless, definitely not marriage material. She was willing to send her pretty, useless boyfriend to go seduce this girl. Again, she switched to English on the word "seduce."

Dinner was over by this point. Glen smiled. "Want me to go?"

"Didn't you understand?" Nini retorted.

"I heard enough. Seduction and parricide." Glen cleared away the plates, giving them the sinister smile of a private detective.

Hongmei said she wasn't interested, and she'd changed her email address anyway. Nini said animatedly that the truth was going to come out soon.

"Stop messing around," said Hongmei. "This person found a picture of a girl online and pretended to be her, and you fell for it."

Nini said at the very least they ought to find out the name of the girl who killed her father, then Google articles about her.

Hongmei said, "That's enough. Stop being crazy. If you really have nothing better to do, go join in the antiwar protest."

On the tenth day after she cut the secret talker from her life, Hongmei was in a terrible mood from writing her thesis and had given up—she was slumped in her swivel chair, playing solitaire. It was late at night. Her feet scrabbled beneath the desk for her slippers. She was chewing a half-eaten apple, thinking it was time for bed. A minute later, she realized she was staring at her inbox.

A message from a name she didn't recognize.

Her heart seemed to stop beating; her lungs felt stuffed full. She didn't know if she was more afraid of the secret talker or of the self that these prying eyes would see through. Her listlessness these last few days had been because she was missing this person's secret words.

Don't ask how I got your new email address. I've known for a while how to break into your artificial sanctuary, but I didn't. I wanted to see whether, if I didn't have you, I could still drink coffee, read the papers, watch TV, listen to music, breathe, eat . . . live. I also wanted to see, if you didn't have me, how you'd behave, speak, look around. Who would you make eyes at? It's been ten days, and the conclusion is that you and I can't do without each other, especially you. In these ten days, you've done everything as usual, but your soul is gone.

Hongmei wanted to snap back, How could you be so shameless and full of yourself? But she didn't. This was not the time to be quibbling about who was chasing whom.

I knew you wouldn't give up so easily. Let's do this properly and set up a meeting. Then we can talk to our hearts' content and know exactly where we stand. We'll take it from there. I could never love a woman, just as I could never be friends with a man.

Are you so sure you couldn't accept a woman?

One hundred percent.

So let's say I'm a man, the way I first appeared—wealthy, idle, eclectically well informed, enough for some gentlemanly embellishments in my conversation. Could you accept a man like that?

I don't know what you're babbling about.

You must. Actually, you've never fully believed that I was a woman. This evening at eight I'll wait for you at the Blue Danube. If you want to tell me to go to hell, you might as well come say it to my face.

10

The Blue Danube coffee shop was where the students hung out. The restaurants on either side closed at nine each night, after which they could come here for a $1.80 soup or a mini pizza for two bucks. Almost every night there'd be students here performing jazz or chamber music. She accepted the secret talker's invitation. What could anyone do in the Blue Danube? Eight o'clock was the busiest time, and every table would be packed.

She got home early from the library and, seeing Glen's leather shoes at the front door, called out, "Hello." Alarmingly, she sounded like a madwoman. Glen called back from his study, "Hello," as if he hadn't noticed anything out of the ordinary. She changed and put on an apron, yelling that she'd be in charge of dinner.

She got some vegetables and a half carton of frozen shrimp from the fridge. There wasn't enough time for it to thaw, so she tossed the frozen brick into the sink, intending to fill the carton with hot water. An ominous thud. When she looked, there were numerous tiny cracks in the sink's white porcelain surface.

Bad things were starting to happen.

She turned on the faucet, and water spurted out, splashing her full in the face. She twisted her head left and right, wiping her face dry on her shoulders, and found she was laughing crazily.

Time to set out the plates, cutlery, and napkins. She dashed back and forth, into the dining room, opening the kitchen door, then forgetting what she'd come to get, climbing the pantry ladder, then forgetting what she'd wanted. Yet she found a lightness and agility she seldom possessed, chopping vegetables with balletic grace. Turning around, she saw Glen at the kitchen door, smiling silently at her. He looked like he'd been watching her for quite a while. She quickly sobered up. There was still time to cancel her appointment with the secret talker, but she knew she wasn't going to do that. She simpered at Glen, despairing at her own shallowness.

Every girlish smile has its consequences. Glen came over and hugged her. She said, "The stove . . . the fire . . ."

A clap of thunder. A long, long time ago storms had loved this place, then there'd been a six-year drought. Now, bit by bit, the rain was coming back.

As if he knew about her secret assignation and was trying to prevent it, Glen hugged her more tightly. She gently stroked his fingers, her mouth full of soothing words. There was no choice—she had to make this appointment, and neither Glen nor the weather would stop her.

Hongmei spent all of dinner silently watching the clock as it ticked closer and closer to eight. Glen seem so innocent, so unperturbed, and chatted aimlessly about classes. He had no idea what she was thinking or plotting. When Glen got up from his seat, leaving his dirty plate and utensils behind, Hongmei saw her chance. Not even bothering to make up an excuse or finish her dinner, she dashed out into the storm, calling out to Glen as he made himself comfortable in front of the TV, "Back soon!"

— — —

There was no one she knew in the Blue Danube. All twenty-odd tables were full, and an experimental play was taking place on the little stage: a dozen theater majors wearing the white face makeup of mimes, imitating the movements of various animals. The lead actor was reciting lines that sounded like they were from *Waiting for Godot*.

Hongmei waited and waited for the secret talker to show up. The scent of rain and hot coffee mingled, making this first encounter feel warmer and more homely. She felt strangely safe.

Her eyes swept across the faces at every table. This person was late. There were no seats she liked the look of, so she went around the walls studying the oil paintings— the handiwork of art majors. The person had said he'd be holding an art journal with a bust by Julio González on the cover. This person had toyed with her enough, playing with both their identity and their gender. She looked at her watch—only one minute had passed. She'd give it ten minutes and then she'd leave. The oil paintings had been hung recently; the paint still smelled fresh. Why not open by saying something about them? People needed safe topics of conversation when they met for the first time. She'd say, Look at these lifeless brushstrokes, these screaming colors that have nothing to say. Just as so much sumptuous-looking food has no taste, or so much sex has no emotion, or so much conversation has no meaning.

She pretended to be absorbed in the paintings and gradually turned a corner. This led her to a passageway that ended at the back door. She guarded the way out, listening to everyone's entrances and exits, movements and silences. Her face was tilted up, her back and neck very relaxed, hands folded lazily before her chest. From the back, she didn't look expectant at all. Now and then a drop of water trickled down from her wet hair, rolling lazily down her temple, leaving a ticklish, icy trail.

Then a new customer walked in, volubly greeting the two girls sitting by the entrance.

It was Glen.

Hongmei retreated into the shadows. So Glen was meeting his students here. Not a good idea, bantering with them like this. Their laughter sounded tense. Glen made more jokes, but these landed even less well. They started talking about schoolwork, and Glen grew more natural. Hemingway, Faulkner, Fitzgerald, O'Neill, Poe, Lowry—geniuses who had succumbed to alcohol. Not just more natural, he was aglow. Hongmei almost forgot this was her husband. She'd never seen him so animated before. The candle on the table gave him a classical profile. It appeared his eyes could easily turn romantic.

The students asked their professor to please speak more slowly so they could take notes.

Hongmei thought these two young girls were already captivated by Glen, though he wasn't doing it on purpose. The angle of the wall cut them off from view, so she could stand there eavesdropping freely, listening as Glen imparted his knowledge, humor, and charisma to these students, as well as a subtle sensuality. Sexual tension was solidifying over their heads, creating a current that sent sparks flying. Hongmei envied those girls a little.

Someone burst out of the bathroom, almost crashing into her. They said sorry at the same time, then stood staring at each other.

Hongmei slipped out of the Blue Danube's back door, having inadvertently proven her supposition: Doesn't everyone live within a triangular relationship? Whether real or fake. She walked through the rain, sprinting ahead like a startled bird. Glen must be keeping an eye on her. Even she was finding her behavior over the last few days suspicious.

Then she stopped abruptly, standing in the school field as the rain poured down on her. She remembered the man who'd come out of the bathroom. He'd smiled at her as he'd apologized. That wasn't a stranger's smile. He was in his forties, sure, just as he'd described himself, not too tall, but well built and proportioned. Dressed in a black lambswool sweater with a high collar that showed off his physique—he probably enjoyed tennis or swimming. His movements were still somewhat boyish, although his hair was starting to go gray. She hesitated, wondering if she ought to go back. But what would she say to Glen? That she was meeting her online lover? She turned to glance at the bustling coffee shop, but her feet didn't move. Their eyes had met, yes, and the description matched. His mouth had opened, as if to speak. She thought that he must be the sort of man who seldom said anything but had a lot of words inside.

Soaked, she got home to find Glen had left her a note.

Two of his doctoral students needed to see him urgently, so they were meeting at the Blue Danube. He didn't sound suspicious of her; his writing was neat and clear. She took off her wet clothes and wrapped herself in a soft towel. All of a sudden she was ravenous. All she'd had for dinner was a few mouthfuls of vegetables. Slapping a slice of cheese on some multigrain bread, she chewed away as she went online.

His message was waiting for her.

He said he knew she must be very disappointed, to have gone out in the rain for nothing. He'd seen her come in from the storm, looking just like a young girl ready to sacrifice herself for love, so determined yet so unbearably delicate. The rain had dissolved her mascara, leaving two dark circles around her eyes, and a skein of damp hair plastered beside her severe mouth. He never knew he was capable of such tender affection, quietly blossoming within him. He remembered she was from a small village, the one where two hundred thirteen girls had died in a single night. Those virgins had collectively sacrificed themselves, for the lovers they hadn't met yet. And so they hadn't had to get married, hadn't been let down, had avoided the twisty road of sin down which wives seek affairs. They simply had died for their potential lovers.

So you left the small village and came in my direction. I watched you standing in the doorway. I was thinking,

What if there were a haystack behind you, a lover's grave? You talked about the boy who came to the village, the one who liked cursing and playing the harmonica—he was buried in an unusual grave too. That's the place you left, a small village like that.

Hongmei wanted to reach out and touch these words, the way they were touching her. She understood what he meant by tender affection.

He said she'd walked past table after table, and it had been obvious even through her clothes that she was breathing hard. The storm had brought out the fear, sleeplessness, and need for alcohol that had been plaguing her for days. It was almost as if this whole affair had become an addiction for her. He'd wanted to come over and embrace her, and tell her how much he regretted his actions. He oughtn't to have frightened her like that. He'd asked for a new beginning, starting with bodily warmth and breath. If Glen hadn't been there, he'd certainly have gotten things started properly with her. She'd fled in such a panic, not even noticing that she'd lost her shawl. He'd picked it up—it still held the warmth and scent of her body.

Hongmei's hands flew to her shoulders, which were empty. Her favorite shawl had fallen into his hands.

He told her not to worry; he'd take good care of it till their next meeting.

She was no longer conjuring up an image out of thin air.

Loving words and the middle-aged man who'd flashed past her combined together. Even this affection was the love of a cowboy, half a smile peeping out from under the brim of a hat, not taking you particularly seriously, but ready to die for you in the blink of an eye. That's fine—that's what she wanted. This was a man who could rejuvenate all her feelings and desires.

He said he could feel her damp body wrapped in its soft cotton towel. This was his hand, ripping off the towel. Not a gentle unwrapping but a firm tug, a bold move, a quick gesture—don't you dare be shy. This was his palm, rubbing against her flesh, this yellow, childlike skin.

He really was making her hot again. Even Glen felt different to her now.

11

While Glen was in class, Nini brought over a videotape to share with Hongmei.

The scene opened on an archway with its vermilion bougainvillea. The tip of the fire tower. In the back of her mind, Hongmei knew she had seen this view before, but she just couldn't place it. The beautiful, useless boyfriend entered the frame and rang the bell. The door opened, revealing a twenty-year-old woman's face. The camera drew closer. The girl was just shaking her head. The boy got out his card: his fake press credentials forged by Nini. She glanced at it, shrugged, smiled, and agreed to take a few questions. She was half hidden behind the door, revealing only half her body—she was an old hand at this. She'd dealt with the media since she was seven.

He asked when she first suspected her father might have been innocent.

"Fourteen," she said.

What gave her the idea?

"The letters he left behind. He wrote many of them and handed them to his lawyer, to be mailed to me on important holidays or my birthday. As I got older, the letters became deeper and more complex. He was always guessing my height and weight, how I was doing at school, wanting me to remember how many years it had been since he departed. He even gave me reading lists, then in the next letter would ask if I'd read the books he mentioned. At the end of every letter, he'd ask me to believe that he'd never harmed me, that he'd always love and protect me. On my fourteenth birthday, I got a letter as usual. There was a pair of crystal earrings in the envelope. The sort of baubles a small child might wear. He said when I was seven we were out one day and I insisted he buy me those earrings. He refused, saying children shouldn't wear jewelry. He'd always felt guilty about that. Now that I was fourteen and could wear jewelry, he hoped I'd enjoy these earrings."

At this point, she hung her head.

Then she went on: "I suddenly realized that I'd been tricked by my therapist, that third-rate psychiatrist who was tricked by Freud in turn. The tragedy was, no one meant to do any harm. The psychiatrist wanted to make a breakthrough in her research, and got famous off the back of my case—at the cost of my family's destruction. I hate my mother. She was under a spell, clutching at shadows like my therapist was. You must have seen all the newspapers saying how they brainwashed and controlled me, a girl of seven."

The boyfriend asked, "How did your father die?"

The woman seemed startled. "You're a reporter yet you don't know the basic facts?"

The boyfriend was flustered but covered. "I don't believe the media's sensationalist news."

"You're right not to. If the media hadn't twisted facts and created this atmosphere in society, my father might not have killed himself. So my father's suicide is connected to their irresponsibility."

"How did he do it?"

"The police found his car deep in the New Mexico desert, with an empty sleeping pill bottle in it. About a month passed between him not showing up in court and the discovery of the car."

"And the body?"

"Anything could have happened in the desert. There are wild animals and vultures, so perhaps—"

"You live alone now?"

"After my mom remarried, I moved out on my own. The money my dad invested for me had appreciated quite a bit, so I can afford to live in San Francisco."

Close-up: the girl's mischievous smile, her body shrinking a little farther behind the front door.

— — —

This girl reminded Hongmei of someone—but who? She couldn't recall. Those expressions, those gestures, that quick wit, but most of all those eyes—she'd seen them all somewhere before. On the video, the door shut. The vermilion bougainvillea and fire tower remained as they were.

Nini said, "Not bad, right? I miked up the boy and bribed an old guy next door to let us shoot from his kitchen window."

Hongmei said, "I didn't ask you to secretly film her!"

"That useless, pretty boy of mine dug up all the information about her—there are dozens of articles online, all of them about that incest case! Even the *New York Times* and *Wall Street Journal* wrote about her! Her father was a rich guy—not too rich, though. The court case bankrupted him—it went on for three years. It was the Child Protective Services that brought charges against him. The chief witnesses were the psychiatrist and the girl's mother."

Hongmei was still wondering where she'd seen that girl before. She told Nini that this whole thing had nothing to do with the secret talker.

Nini had nothing to say to that. She had indeed wandered down a different rabbit hole.

Even so, Hongmei was dimly aware that the secret talker must have had some reason for stealing this girl's identity to talk to Nini.

At eleven later that night, she got another message saying he'd expected her to be at the Blue Danube, but she hadn't shown up. He was using the coffee shop's Wi-Fi to email her and would wait there until they closed.

She glanced at her watch. Half an hour to closing time. She quickly changed her clothes and combed her hair, then hurried out the door. Glen usually stayed in his study till midnight, and she'd be back before that. But as she opened the front door, she hesitated—this seemed too risky. She left Glen a note saying a friend was visiting from out of town, and she was popping by the campus for a quick chat, back in thirty minutes. The college was full of night owls, so Glen wouldn't find that suspicious. She put the note on the fridge, but as she turned, she heard a clunk as the magnet fell to the floor. For some reason the magnet wasn't cooperating—she kept sticking it back up, and it kept falling. Then she heard a voice: "Its magnetism is used up."

Afterward, she wished she'd managed not to panic. It was just Glen coming out to see what the noise was. But she felt her face stiffen and knew this was bad—no matter what expression she tried to make, it would look hideous.

So instead, she turned back to the fridge and pulled out an open bottle of white wine. Still with her back to Glen, she asked if he'd like a glass.

Seeing how she was dressed, Glen asked if she was going out.

She didn't answer his question, just said that her thesis was almost done, and it felt like her life was ending soon. She knew she was making the situation worse and worse. The note was crumpled in her hand.

Glen said it was so late, maybe she should just stay home.

She could hear the awkwardness in his voice.

She said, "Who says I'm going out?"

"I don't mind you going out. Why are you so defensive?"

"How am I defensive? Anyway, it wouldn't make a difference if you minded. I don't need your permission to do or not do anything."

Her voice was tight, and all sorts of mistakes were creeping into her English, but she didn't care.

Glen stared at his wife in surprise. So she could bare her teeth too. Why was she so agitated? Look, look, that frenzied grin again.

"Well said," Glen replied. "And so your defensiveness is unwarranted."

"I'm telling you, I'm not defensive at all."

Don't be like that, she thought, letting annoyance turn into anger. *It's undignified.* But she couldn't help using the secret talker as a shield. With him around, she wasn't scared of Glen.

He said, "If you insist on going out this late at night, I'm coming with you."

She suddenly screamed, "I'm not going out!"

"I don't mind you going out."

She threw up her hands in resignation, as if she was giving up ever being understood by him. She felt rage against Glen, and tenderness toward the secret talker, who understood her so well, even though they were so far apart. In that moment, she felt duty bound to love this person. She didn't want to be with this husband, standing right in front of her yet separated by such a gulf of communication.

Seeing her start to weep, Glen came over and tried to hug her, but she stepped aside. His arm immediately shrank back respectfully. She waited for him to come closer and ignore her protests, wrap his arms around her. At these times she didn't know what to do. She needed Glen to be a big brother, to protect her unconditionally, to force her to think before acting, to help her to understand that taking one step back would return her to safety and forgiveness. Right now she wanted him to pull her back, prevent her from falling into an uncertain embrace.

But Glen just stood there. He would never get it or give her what she wanted, what she needed.

Finally he said in a reasonable tone, "You wrote me a note. May I read it?"

So he'd seen the crumpled scrap of paper. It was too late now anyway. The Blue Danube was closed by now.

She slapped the note down on the table and said, "I'll go pack."

"Where are you going?"

"I'll get a motel."

"Which one?"

She came out of the bathroom with her toiletry bag. To think he'd actually asked the question. *Which one?!*

"What difference does it make?" she said, pulling bras and panties from the wardrobe in their bedroom. "Are you going to recommend a motel?" She laughed nastily.

"If it's far from here, I'd suggest you wait till tomorrow morning."

He would never be able to understand her.

She concentrated on packing her bag and getting out.

Every line of her body screamed that she had been wronged. In her mind, she urged him to pity her, complained that he was so cruel that he didn't even try to rush over and hold her back, forcing her into his wide and warm chest or blocking the door that stood between a safe haven and deep, unknowable night.

Instead, she was at the front door, despairingly slipping on her shoes, taking as long as she possibly could to give him a chance to say something, to pull her back, and then everyone could go back to normal without losing face. But he was illiterate when it came to her body language, she realized as she put on the second shoe.

She left. No matter how bad this was, she could only keep walking forward.

The elevator crawled up toward her, floor after floor.

Glen appeared behind her, pulling on his coat, the collar twisted inside out.

He said, "It's so late. I'll give you a lift."

She said, "Do you know where I'm going?"

He said, "No matter where you're going, I'm worried you won't be safe." He produced a card. "Here's my AAA membership. It'll get you a discount at most roadside motels."

He looked serious and responsible, without a hint of sarcasm. His collar was rubbing against his neck, and he turned his head uncomfortably. She couldn't help reaching out to straighten it. Now he finally grabbed her hand and pulled it against his chest. She thought Glen's eyes would always stare at her like this, perplexed. He had no idea how, at this moment, she was treating him like a big brother in order to reconcile with him.

Right then she'd wished Glen dead. Looking at the row of knives on their wall, she had thought only these could end the painful differences between them. Maybe she'd kill herself—that would make things a lot simpler. Before the secret talker showed up, before she'd known there was an intelligent person in the world who understood her, she'd never realized what torture it was not to be able to communicate.

She'd never been so utterly disappointed.

She had told the secret talker stories she would never reveal to Glen. She recounted the loss of her baby. Compared to now, even then, she hadn't felt so let down by her marriage.

In her third spring after moving to America, she had discovered she was pregnant. That night, she'd cooked a spread for dinner, setting out red candles and roses. But Glen got home so late that the food was cold and the candles almost burnt out.

He said, "Why did you get red candles? You know I don't like that color."

She was surprised—she'd never seen him looking so awful.

Still, she kept smiling, saying, "This is a good night for red." Red was an auspicious color for the Chinese.

He forced a laugh. "Thank you for making dinner."

He took a sip of wine, then asked why she wasn't drinking.

She said sweetly, "From now on I won't be able to touch alcohol." She waited for him to ask why, but he just started eating and drinking in silence, as if something was on his mind. She asked if the students had annoyed him. He said there wasn't a day when those young idiots didn't make him angry.

She said, "Let's have a baby."

He didn't even look up. "Why?"

"We ought to have a baby," she said, her heart cooling down.

He said he couldn't see why they "ought to."

She said, "Isn't it good to have a child? A family ought to have a child."

"So whatever you do, it's because you 'ought to'?"

She was silent. The red candles flickered listlessly.

Right, so who got to decide what they "ought to" do? Love was no longer enough to bring together these two souls, these two bodies. They needed a child to do that. The baby would provide a new theme, filling their withering days with a new story.

Hongmei had told the secret talker frankly that before she became pregnant, she'd gone for coffee with a male classmate and then accompanied him to a concert in San Francisco. There'd even been a couple of times when they'd stopped at the lights and before driving off when he'd kissed her. He was a Northern European. At that time, Northern Europe still felt mysterious to her.

Before getting pregnant, she had tasted disappointment for the first time. She'd always thought there would be an even bigger world in front of her, an even more perfect man waiting for her love. In the end, this wasn't the case. She had married into the Pacific Coast, giving up everything else. And this was all she had gotten in return. Often, when she was enjoying an ice cream, trying on expensive clothes, or watching the latest movie, her mind would wander into questioning whether this was the bigger, better world she'd wanted, the one she'd sacrificed so much for, causing so much destruction in her pursuit of it. A dull despair would wash over her, and she would toss aside the latest fashions or her favorite ice cream. What should she do with this disillusionment? How could she deal with the melancholy that frequently overtook her? She thought about the educated youth, playing his harmonica on that haystack, his eyes filling with expectation and sadness as he described the most delicious ice cream in the world. If he were still alive, and in her place, would he also be sighing, Is this all there is?

Just as she was at the "Is this all there is?" stage, the baby had shown up.

How many times have children broken a stalemate? In movies both good and bad, babies were always a turning point.

She hadn't expected such a negative response from Glen. She sat there, feeling herself shrinking, just like the red candles, while Glen lectured her about the virtues of childlessness. Lying felt ugly.

She had told the secret talker that up to this point, her disappointment had been hazy and incomprehensible, but in that instant, it had grown concrete. To this day, she still wasn't sure what exactly Glen's objection to babies was. People who don't like children inevitably lack tenderness, and those who don't understand kids are always poor at communication. The secret talker could surely imagine how great her disenchantment had been.

She said nothing. Ten days later, she quietly went for an abortion. The procedure went badly, leaving her bleeding heavily. Not wanting to alarm Glen, she quietly took herself to the ER. The doctor said half the fetus had been left inside her body but would be eliminated naturally. Following his instructions, she collected in a jar everything her body expelled, so the hospital could examine it and make sure the fetal tissue was all gone. The jar stayed hidden in a cardboard box behind the toilet bowl.

Glen noticed it and asked what that bloody mass was.

Her heart filled with vicious swear words. She wanted to say, Isn't that what you wanted? Now we won't have descendants. Or else, Can't you tell? That's the result of us bumping uglies. But instead, she gritted her teeth and just stared at him.

In that moment, she had seen her ex-husband's face, so boyish and yet every inch her husband. When Jianjun had seen her emerge from the abortion room, he'd scooped her up and, just like that, carried her up four flights of stairs, sobbing and cursing all the way, "Quotas, quotas—next time we're having it, quota or no quota."

But then Glen said, "I said I didn't want children, but I didn't ask you to have an abortion."

So he knew. It turned out that Glen had intercepted her mail and seen the hospital bill for the abortion.

He said, "Now that the child was here, I'd have adjusted myself and welcomed him. Why did you have to go against destiny and kill him?"

She screamed, "You're inhuman, inside and out!" She realized she'd started yelling in Chinese. Why was that such a relief? She went on: "Jianjun wouldn't have treated me like this! Jianjun! I let you down!"

She was howling, the way women keened for the dead in her little village.

Glen didn't understand any of this, just stood to one side, murmuring, "It'll be all right, it'll be all right."

She shouted, "Fuck your 'It'll be all right'! You broke me and Jianjun apart. I must have been blind!"

He said, "Everything will be all right."

Later that night, she had gotten up, feeling as weak as wet paper. Finding some aspirin in the medicine cabinet, she thought any pills could kill you if you took enough of them. Standing by the bed, she stared at Glen as he slumbered. She thought, *At least he has no trouble sleeping.* She didn't know how long she stayed there, looking at this American man she'd given everything up to chase after. Twenty-eight years old, not even halfway through her life, and she'd always been the one doing the chasing. She'd never lied about this but would openly declare to all her female friends, "I was the one who pursued him. It wasn't easy to tie him down!"

Look at this happiness she'd chased down.

Jianjun had had his nasty moments too, and at those times she'd also thought: *Look, there's the man I ran after.*

She turned away from the bed, felt dizzy, and crashed to the floor. It was no more than nine yards from the kitchen to the bedroom, but she didn't have the strength to make it even that far. Still clutching the aspirin bottle, she drifted off.

The next morning, she woke up and found she'd changed back to the daytime version of herself—the way others saw her: sensible, sweet-natured, decorous. Daytime her would never have gulped down ten aspirin tablets. As she pulled herself from the confusion of the overdose and returned to Glen's side, she became a different woman.

The same thing happened this time. After running out in the storm, despite Glen's protests, she drove around aimlessly until she was too exhausted to continue without crashing, parked on a side street, and fell asleep. In the morning, she was subdued and returned to Glen's side. And as always, Glen said nothing.

— — —

It's as you said: I'm emotionally repressed. More than ten years ago, I was repressed with Jianjun as well, and it was Glen who opened me up. But now I'm repressed with him.

The secret talker said he'd always known she was a dangerous woman. He had a good eye for women like her. His daughter was dangerous too. In her eyes, the world suddenly became laughable and contemptible.

He had watched her pass between two identical two-story buildings, then through a vast parking lot, her shoulders tilted a little to the left, a habit left over from when she'd carried a rifle on her back. The shopping mall had seven or eight chain stores, five fast food chains, three chain banks, a chain supermarket, and a chain gas station. Like most malls in this country, the walls were painted pale pastel colors, the ceiling a swathe of ocean blue.

What distinguishes America is that it's made up of these indistinguishable chains.

You put a couple of coins into the machine and took a newspaper, the secret talker wrote. Then you froze, staring at the shopping mall in front of you crouching stupidly, hideously on the horizon. What damned architect designed this squat building? You couldn't remember which city you were in; it could have been anywhere in the US. The chain stores crisscrossed the whole country, chaining everyone up, erasing individuality—individuality was dangerous. The chains made everyone march in step, which was easier. The safe, chained people sat, obese, in the setting sun, enjoying the pleasure of not communicating. Talking carried too much risk. How many people could survive the cut and thrust of conversation, the pinprick of truth? How strong, how intelligent, how positive would the survivors need to be? Look how secure people are in the embrace of chains. Even the pigeons seemed at ease, waddling happily around the outdoor seating. This scene was absurd, hideous. You suddenly remembered how hard you'd chased after this more than a decade ago. The last time you went back to your hometown, you told the children that America had countless malls, each the size of the little village. That kind of material excess was beyond those children's imagination.

His words were filled with a disgust that hadn't been there before.

He said Hongmei had changed her mind at the supermarket entrance, taking a step back after the automatic doors had opened for her, turning right and heading into Starbucks instead. There was an eight-foot-long bulletin board there, where people put up notes advertising rooms for rent, secondhand goods, or private classes. Lamps from the forties were being sold as antiques. He saw Hongmei reach out to grab a slip of paper with a landlord's phone number on it, but soon after that she stuck it back, turning to another ad. This one was right at the bottom, not very noticeable. It had a picture of a hunting dog, so he thought it must be for a pet obedience school. Hongmei knelt down, her hand resting against the wall, to see the text more clearly. The words were jammed together, a dense black mass covering half the paper.

He had seen Hongmei rip off the last little paper tag hanging from the bottom—the other nineteen were already gone. She held it in her palm and studied it, head tilted to one side. When a gust of wind blew it away, she took a couple of steps after it, then stopped, watching it twist and turn, flying far away. When he had looked back at her face, it seemed she'd had a new thought.

After she left, he'd gone over to look at the hunting dog ad. It wasn't anything to do with animals, it turned out, but an advertisement for a retired private investigator. He or she taught a method of vanishing from the people who knew you. Anyone with a past they wanted to leave behind could use this tactic to start anew. And if you were tired of your marriage or your profession, this was also the cheapest, least harmful way to leave. If you were tired of yourself and wanted a brand-new personality, this gave you the best chance of achieving that. And of course, it made life a lot easier for men who wanted to become women, or vice versa. An eight-week course (an hour and a half per week) and a thousand dollars in fees was all you needed to end your previous identity and start all over again.

He told Hongmei that in 1992, the *San Francisco Chronicle* had run an article about the phenomenon of people vanishing, mentioning several books that told you how to do it. By 1993, more than seventy thousand people had disappeared nationwide. Some had been in debt, some had committed murder, some had been accused of a crime with no way to prove their innocence, some had been enmeshed in affairs they couldn't free themselves from. These people had carefully planned every step of their disappearance, acquiring new birth certificates, IDs, and Social Security numbers, then one night or one early morning, they had vanished forever. Some had faked their own suicide or murder; others had left behind sincere goodbye letters.

Imagine how these seventy thousand people were now. Whether their vanishing had brought them pain or joy, it had surely opened up a vast unknown world to them.

Of these seventy thousand, some had gone abroad, where they became adventurers or language teachers. The Far East was ideal for this. Take China—newly liberated, naive about the West . . . Can you imagine? Perhaps among your foreign professors there was a member of the vanished, someone who'd become too disppointed in others or in himself.

Hongmei looked at that word, "disppointed," spelled wrongly for the twenty-third time.

He said he'd been watching her through binoculars, but when she had gotten to the shopping mall, she hadn't known where she was going.

She felt a little uneasy. Why was he always lurking in the dark, leaving her unprepared for their encounters?

He seemed to sense the anguish she wasn't expressing and said he was very sorry, he knew he was always flaking out at the last minute, afraid of letting her down if he came out from behind the shield of words, by being just an ordinary man. He confessed to using extra-powerful binoculars to bring her closer to himself, examining her detail by detail. This way, he could own her body, inch by inch, kissing her bit by bit. Her underdeveloped breasts were mesmerizing to him; the birthmark on her ass filled him with savage desire.

She gaped at these words. How had he seen that birthmark? Had she revealed it while she was swimming? But she did her laps first thing in the morning, when there were hardly any people at the pool.

He said he knew this sort of obsession was unhealthy,

but he couldn't help it. He wanted her to believe that he understood love, both spiritual and physical.

The binoculars pulled you into my arms. Feel my chest—broad enough for you? My shoulders—firm enough? My skin, which smells like I've been out in the sun. My body is warm. Your hands feel cool against it. Parched skin beneath them. And these are your eyes, black and inviting. Inviting sympathy, understanding, even invasion. And so you brought this on yourself. You can't escape now. Invasion always hurts a little. Now you'll open yourself up and accept me.

Hongmei was breathing hard. She blazed as she read these words, hating herself for being so useless, and hating him for luring her down this evil path. Did she really hate him? She couldn't work it out.

He told her to meet him in a neighborhood in San Francisco called South of Market, in a bar called The EndUp. He said he owned a little apartment with a terrace in the city with a beautiful view, and if she wanted, he could invite her over. He didn't want her to feel scared. The EndUp was very trendy and always packed with men and women flirting with each other. He and she could have a proper conversation there, or they could just flirt, or not flirt. This was a place where you could be serious or casual.

She left a note on the refrigerator saying that she was going to San Francisco to meet a couple of friends from

China and would be back late. Glen had also left a folded note for her, but she didn't read it and just put it in her pocket. Seeing Glen's writing would weaken her. She couldn't lose her resolve.

She drove for almost two hours, arriving and finally finding parking in the South of Market district at three in the afternoon. The antiwar protest had created traffic congestion, blocking the entrance to office buildings, so the workers trying obediently to get to their jobs were now waiting in the streets for the police to escort them inside in small groups. She remembered Nini saying she was coming into town with dozens of students, and she started scanning the crowds. Sure enough, there was Nini on Market Street. She and her boyfriend were both in white T-shirts, smeared with red paint to look like blood, a gory sight at first glance. Nini had recently become a bit of a heroine within the movement and was frequently interviewed on TV.

"Did Glen come with you?" she yelled.

Hongmei lied, saying Glen had classes and couldn't come.

"I just saw him!" Nini turned to her boyfriend. "Isn't that right? He was standing over there, taping it."

Hongmei's heart went *boom*. Glen must be secretly watching her.

Nini said she wanted to eat fruit with shaved ice and

dragged Hongmei and her boyfriend into a shop. When they saw her "bloodstained" shirt, everyone started yelping in shock. Nini nonchalantly told her boyfriend to get the desserts and then turned back to chat with Hongmei. She said her boyfriend had almost fallen madly in love with the girl who'd destroyed her father. But, by the way, she could make one thing clear: the girl spelled "disappointment" correctly, which is to say the secret talker had indeed just been making use of her identity.

Now that Nini was a star of the antiwar movement, all the tycoons in every industry had seen her getting led away by the police, singing "The Internationale" sweetly at the camera. Not one of them would go out with her now.

Hongmei asked if she still wanted to marry a rich man.

She said she felt differently now that she was a revolutionary, as if a different set of hormones had started flowing through her body. She no longer found millionaires sexy, just as in the past when she hadn't found poor men attractive, even if they were handsome. She said whatever got her blood going was good—that's all she needed.

Hongmei said goodbye to Nini and her boyfriend and plunged into the crowd of protesters. Her brain worked swiftly, trying to decide what she should say if she bumped into Glen. She knew she must look ridiculous and decided this would be the last time—after this she would tell Glen everything.

She glanced at her watch. It was still an hour till her meeting with the secret talker. She'd deliberately gotten here early, to give herself time to scope out the area and make sure she had an escape route. She was five blocks from The EndUp, and the walk would give her time to steady herself. She got out her compact mirror and lipstick, which was the trendiest shade and made her mouth look soft and moist. As she put her compact back into her purse, her hand bumped against another object: a toothbrush. She'd actually brought a toothbrush. All the contradictory plans she'd made had included spending the night here. She pressed her fingers against the bristles and rubbed hard, thinking, *Let's see how wild this woman gets today.* Driving for two hours to meet a man from the internet. And after that? Would he take advantage of the singer hitting a long note to grab her hand and pull her from the nightclub, a woman who came with her own toothbrush?

On the way to The EndUp, she found herself wishing it was farther away, to give her more time to think.

In her last email she'd told him a story from her childhood that no one else knew.

By late fall, the children had stopped going to the haystacks in the evenings to hear the city boy play his harmonica. Only one eleven-year-old girl would show up every day. The boy would play his harmonica for her, and she became the only recipient of his complaints about the little village. One evening the streetlights were coming on and the voices of women rose and fell as they called their children home, a beguiling scene. The boy slid down the haystack, wiping his harmonica against his trousers. Suddenly, he stopped moving and just stared at the girl. She smiled, not finding this strange. He reached out with both hands and grabbed her waist, then lowered her to the ground from the haystack, ending up face-to-face with her. The girl could hear her mother calling for her. She didn't answer, just twisted her head away. When she turned back, she no longer recognized the person in front of her. His eyes were almost shut behind his glasses, though not tightly, the whites gleaming faintly between his lowered lids. His lashes trembled violently. She'd never seen such droopy eyelashes. She called his name twice, and he smiled terrifyingly, pressing his lips to her forehead. She started pushing away his hands, and her legs resisted too, though she made sure to keep a smile on her face, as if it would be too much to shame him. His lips were scalding hot as he pressed them to hers, and for a moment she had no idea if this sensation was good or bad. She could smell Donghai cigarettes on his breath, spicy and bitter, a masculine scent, permeating her body. A peculiar lack of strength opened her whole body to him, melding with the tobacco fragrance. She wondered if she ought to run away or scream, but then her lips were forced apart by something. It took her a long while to realize it was his tongue. Then he slowly pulled her beneath the haystack. Someone had hollowed out a space here. She could barely move. He curled around her body.

Afterward, he pulled her out and got her to stand up so he could straighten her clothes and brush the straw from her hair. He smiled awkwardly. There was nothing scary in this smile. She looked at him, a secret emotion appearing in the darkness of her body, like a tiny flame. He asked her to come back the next night at the same time. She nodded and turned to go. She couldn't make out whether she liked or didn't like this sort of thing, nor did she understand what on Earth the city boy had just done to her. He'd lit a flame inside her body, and it was filling her with warmth.

The next night, she came back to the haystack. The boy had turned the hollow into a nesting cave, and he told the girl they had nothing to be afraid of, not even if it rained or the wind turned cold.

The third night, the boy was startled awake by some noise. When he peeped out the window of his house, he saw all the men in the village circling it, holding up hoes and pickaxes. He fled out the back window and found all the streets and alleyways full of people. Sixty or seventy dogs were barking at the same time. He could hide himself only in the hollow he'd made. The villagers stuck pitchforks into every haystack.

Afterward, they lit them all on fire. The boy from the city didn't come out.

The villagers said he'd seduced six or seven girls in their early teens. In order to protect their reputations, they were never named. These girls had been too greedy, the towns-people said. They'd gone into the haystack with him for a paltry piece of candy. The eleven-year-old girl thought what had happened between him and her was more than just a piece of candy. He'd never offered her anything in return for those kisses and caresses. By the time he was pulled out from the smoldering ashes, the pale-faced student had become a human-shaped lump of charcoal. Only the har-monica had survived intact.

His descriptions of foreign countries now seemed com-pletely wrong. But this was what the little girl had aspired to as she grew up. From the age of eleven, she had known for sure that she would travel farther than any other woman from their village—farther than those girls who'd ended up working in cotton mills in Shanghai or Nanjing, farther than the women who'd left with the land reform brigades in the fifties, farther than those who'd gotten into Tongji University in the sixties. She was the only female student for hundreds of miles around, in thousands of years, to get a place in the Military Academy of Foreign Languages. She was sixteen years old, the youngest candidate.

That girl was Hongmei.

Before meeting in person, Hongmei wanted to tell the secret talker her deepest secrets so this relationship could be built with the highest degree of honesty. Their beginning would be different, no longer full of beautiful misunderstandings or lies. She had told him this and wanted him to see what sort of creature she was, always giving in to emotion. The longings of her heart and flesh were more important to her than truth or falsehood, love or hate. She finally felt free.

12

It was only half past six when she got to The EndUp. Half an hour to while away. She decided to go to a nearby hotel with a dimly lit bar. A pianist was playing in the lobby, which soothed her quite a bit, at least temporarily. A waiter glided over and asked in a hushed voice what she'd like to drink. She grinned wildly and said a Bloody Mary. She drank very slowly, as if this could stretch out the time before her fall. There was no going back now.

It was almost seven, but the summer night was still far away. She opened her purse but found her wallet missing. In her romantic frenzy, she'd packed a toothbrush but not her wallet. She looked around for the waiter and saw him busy chatting with another couple of guests. Summoning all her old military skill and training, she slipped out behind his back.

Having successfully ducked the bar bill, she wandered tipsily on. He must already be inside, hoping to actually get his hands on his prey this time. She stumbled toward his trap. Armed only with a toothbrush, she was heading for a beautiful, if hygienic, night. The waiter must have noticed she was gone by now and must be thinking that a woman like her was too old to be dodging a bill. She thought, *What a mess I am, doing two dastardly things in one night.*

Was Glen searching for her now? Never in his life would he imagine she'd be so depraved as to come to The EndUp, a place where people stripped off their pale human skins to show the monsters within. The EndUp—a good name. Two hosts, dressed all in black, came toward her to ask if she had a reservation. There weren't many people inside, but the secret talker was surely already waiting.

The hosts came even closer and said very distinctly, "Do. You. Have. A. Reservation?"

The alcohol was getting to her. She could smell the musky scent of a wild animal pursuing her, with a hint of bougainvillea.

She could feel Glen's note crinkle in her pocket. Suddenly, the smells, the alcohol, the note, unlocked the final piece of the puzzle—she understood the whole situation. She turned and ran, her leather sandals going tap, tap against the sidewalk, like another person's footsteps. She thought of Glen's eyes. The same eyes set in a much younger and female face—the girl in the pictures Nini had sent to her. How could she have been so dense? She should have pieced together everything much earlier. Maybe she hadn't wanted to know the truth. Living with secrets had become the norm, her natural state. She got to the parking lot, keys already in her hand, and a minute later was roaring out onto the road.

She found the archway surrounded by vermilion bougainvillea. So many years ago, nearly a decade, Glen had taken her here, a walk on his favorite street he had claimed— perhaps he had wanted to confess something then. That was why this place had looked so familiar to her. They had walked over the bougainvillea leaves, holding hands as one. As time passed and they shifted apart, she'd forgotten it. Maybe she hadn't been fair to Glen either, hadn't listened to him or paid attention to his feelings. Maybe if she had, she would've known the truth all along; she wouldn't have been a disappointment too. But now, bolstered by her new-found clarity, she rushed over, and sure enough, the tip of the fire tower was visible diagonally behind it. Such attractive surroundings didn't match the nefarious reasons she'd invited herself here. She rang the bell and heard a woman's footsteps crossing a little courtyard, coming to the outer door. The peephole was about the size of a fist, revealing a youthful face. "Who are you?" asked the woman, but then recognition flickered in her familiar eyes.

Hongmei beamed. She couldn't smile so warmly if she were sober.

"I was looking for you." She said the woman's name.

Two more people appeared in the courtyard, one male and one female, about the woman's age.

Hongmei was invited in. They'd been having dinner—half a pizza was still piping hot in its take-out box, and three beer bottles stood empty. She quickly said, "I'm so sorry to disturb your meal."

"Would you like to join us?" said the woman, polite but distant, just like her father.

Hongmei recognized at once the shawl on the living room sofa. She walked over, one step, two steps, three steps, heel, toe, heel . . . bent down, reached out. The embroidery on the shawl, which she'd bought so many years ago, just before leaving the little village, on a day that happened to have a temple festival. She'd stitched this piece of embroidery onto an ordinary wool shawl and had made a unique garment. But how had it ended up here? By the time she turned around, to face this long-lost daughter, she'd decided what to say.

"I was supposed to meet your father elsewhere, but I came here."

The woman stared at her. Finally, she opened her mouth.

"I know who you are. He talks about you a lot."

Hongmei's hands were still running over the shawl as she looked at the girl's eyes. Weren't they the same familiar eyes that had shone on her every day from the most intimate perspectives? How could have she missed it? How could she have missed the same grayish blue, the same deep folds, the same slight weariness from having seen too much?

She found herself saying, "I didn't expect you to be all grown up."

"It's been more than ten years since that awful affair."

"Twelve years since he vanished."

"He told you everything?"

"In a way, yes." Hongmei smiled. "In the most impossible way."

The girl smiled too. "He's an impossible father."

The woman looked pained for a moment but immediately pulled a face and smiled again.

Hongmei thought with some emotion that even with all the mystery and lies, there had been sincerity in this shared father-daughter pain after all.

"Why not publicly acknowledge your father? He could come out of hiding."

"He only got in touch with me two months ago."

Hongmei thought, *That's right*. He had talked about reuniting with his daughter a couple of months ago. That had sounded made-up, but it actually had happened.

"We'd have to make a lot of arrangements first," said the woman. "How to deal with the media, and my mother . . . We'll have to plan everything thoroughly. To my father and me, this was a total catastrophe. We're too battle-scarred to be able to defend ourselves against the media and all the public figures who'll line up to attack us again."

The woman's huge, deep eyes had fine lines around them. Hongmei thought, *They even wrinkle in the same way*, these old-seeming eyes.

As the woman said goodbye, she said not to worry. Her father would definitely wait for Hongmei—he indulged the women he loved. The woman raised an eyebrow, trying to look cheeky, but her wounds had brought her preternatural maturity, so her expression was at odds with her face.

"You understand my father better than I do. You know how much he'll give in to you," she said.

"Huh. That's not how it felt in his messages. He was always distant. Everything was a secret." Hongmei paused, smiling a little. "He writes well, though, apart from not being able to spell the word 'disappointed.'"

"Missing the letter *a*? Yeah, he always gets that wrong. Maybe there's some special reason. You should ask him."

Hongmei pulled the shawl around her shoulders and headed back outside. As she opened her car door, the woman smiled and waved. That smile was so familiar, it made Hongmei dizzy.

She drove through the city center. There were long lines of candles on either side of the street and people singing "Give Peace a Chance."

A short Asian man holding a wooden sign, speaking

loudly, kept flickering in and out of view in the candle-light. He was a professional protester—no matter what the cause, he'd turn up with that placard, saying the same thing, standing earnestly among the crowds. He was like the professional mourners in Hongmei's home village, except he wasn't getting paid. Enmities and alliances would transform, the power balance would shift, and national governments would fall—but he was eternal, unchanging.

Hongmei navigated the crowded streets with difficulty, finally returning to the south side. It was almost nine. Even so, he was surely still waiting in The EndUp. Her heart was full of tenderness for this poor, wounded soul. She was a gentle pacifist on this antiwar night. No matter who became enemies with whom the next day, or who made up with whom, she wouldn't change; she would be eternal and go on loving.

She parked the car and walked toward The EndUp. This area grew abandoned after dark, apart from drunkards lounging on the steps of closed factories and shops. She walked down the street, seeing The EndUp in the distance like a mirage. Even this road felt wild and dangerous, the silence before an ambush.

It was ten past nine. Her footsteps were steady and determined, this person late for an appointment. No need to retreat again.

Ten paces from The EndUp.

In the entryway of the bar, she finally pulled out the note that Glen had left for her on the fridge. She stood in the dimness, with the note in her palm, and read every word as if it were the first time she had truly paid attention to Glen's words.

> Hongmei, I am afraid I'm a constant
> disppointment to you. There's something
> important I need to say to you, Glen.

There it was, the omission between *s* and *p*. Not only a missing letter: so many things had gone missing from their smooth, inert married life, one after another, over the years. The courage with which they had overcome impossible obstacles a decade ago in her far-off homeland had long since disappeared. They had no capacity to dive deeper into the stormy waters of their feelings, choosing to hurt in silence, in secret. But maybe now with the lies peeled away, it could be different.

She stepped through the doorway.

ABOUT THE AUTHOR

Geling Yan is one of the most acclaimed contemporary novelists and screenwriters writing in the Chinese language today. She published her first novel in 1986 and since then has written over twenty books and won over thirty awards. Her works have been translated into twelve languages; several have been adapted for screen. She has also worked with directors like Zhang Yimou and Ang Lee. She currently divides her time between Berlin and China.

Here ends Geling Yan's
The Secret Talker.

The first edition of this book was printed and
bound at LSC Communications in
Harrisonburg, Virginia, April 2021.

A NOTE ON THE TYPE

The text of this novel was set in ITC Legacy Serif,
a typeface designed by Ronald Arnholm in the
early 1990s. Arnholm, then a graduate student
at Yale, drew inspiration from Nicolas Jenson's
(1420–1480) early Roman typefaces. ITC Legacy
maintains the beauty and elegance of Jenson's
original, while improving legibility with its open
counters and clean character shapes.

HARPERVIA

An imprint dedicated to publishing international voices,
offering readers a chance to encounter other lives and other
points of view via the language of the imagination.